The Star Shack

The Star Shack

LILA CASTLE

Published by Sourcebooks Fire, an imprint of Sourcebooks, Inc.
P.O. Box 4410, Naperville, Illinois 60567-4410
(630) 961-3900
Fax: (630) 961-2168
teenfire.sourcebooks.com

Library of Congress Cataloging-in-Publication data is on file with the publisher.

Printed and bound in the United States of America.
VP 10 9 8 7 6 5 4 3 2 1

Annabelle Lomax

Born August 20: Leo ♌

Rising Sign: Aquarius ♒

You are passionate and dramatic in life and in love. Once you find that special person, you are loyal, sometimes to a fault. You are a fire sign best paired with others whose devotion burns bright: Leos, Sagittarians, and Arians.

chapter 1

The first time I saw Annabelle Lomax, she was holding a gun.

It was pointed straight at the enemy of every single middle-schooler who ever spent summers at Gingerbread Beach. That enemy was Laser Tag Larry—and, yeah, the gun was just a laser-tag gun—but it's hard not to emphasize the drama of the moment. This was *Laser Tag Larry.*

When I saw Annabelle gripping the plastic pistol, her single wild curls flying out behind her, I knew (shut up; it's embarrassing enough to admit) my life had changed forever. Not that I'm one of those corny people who believes in love at first sight or soul mates or any of that stuff.

I'm definitely not. But three facts: 1) I was suddenly sweating even though it was cold and rainy on the boardwalk; 2) I couldn't take my eyes off her; 3) I'd forgotten about the game of laser tag my friend Scott had challenged me to. At twelve, nothing matters more than a laser-tag challenge. Nothing.

Hence the drama of pointing a gun at Laser Tag Larry. No one does drama quite like Annabelle Lomax.

• • •

The quiet thud of a raindrop hits the roof of my old silver Honda. The sun is still shining behind me, but the dark clouds directly ahead mean I'm getting close. I can't help stepping on the gas just a little harder, even though I promised my mom I'd keep to the speed limit if my parents let me drive down from Vermont on my own in our other car. My parents are ski instructors, so you'd think they'd be fiends for land speed, but actually my mom is a paranoid control freak.

I made sure to stop for gas right away so they couldn't tail me. Not that my parents are so bad, but I didn't want to spend the four hours driving to Gingerbread Beach hearing about the article my mom is writing on ski gear for *Ski Now* and having her gasp and reach for the door handle every time I passed another vehicle.

Instead, I wanted to spend the time listening to my iPod. I don't have anything against other music besides the triumvirate (Sex Pistols, The Clash, and the Ramones), but really, no one says it quite like old-school '70s punk. With my friends, I'll listen to rap or whatever, but when I'm alone, I like the classics.

So once I ditch my parents at the gas station, it's just me and Joey Ramone. At first, I'm mostly singing along, banging the steering wheel. But then the live version of "I Want to be Your Boyfriend" comes on, and it gets me thinking about the summer.

Before the spring, I was practically counting down the days to June 25 when we'd head back to our summer house in Gingerbread with the endless rain that's a million times better than all the snow we get at home—see, rain has the added perk of keeping tourists away at a beach resort—and the boardwalk where Jed makes the best coffee ever at the Opera House Café. Where you can get a bucket of clams at Kitty's Clam Shack next door, so fresh they are practically still breathing. But really it's Annabelle. At least it always was Annabelle until a few months ago.

The rain is steady now. When I turn on my wipers, I remember that I was supposed to get new ones before the trip. No big deal; I'm almost there—and I know the route by heart since we've been coming here since I was in seventh grade. And although I'm not sure how things will go with Annabelle, if this really will be the summer we finally get together, I can't help smiling like a lunatic when I see the sign—GINGERBREAD BEACH SCENIC DRIVE 1 MILE—up ahead.

Once I exit the highway, I'm really feeling it. I roll down the window, and the rain pelts the passenger seat, mixing with the salty smell of the ocean. I pass the Everything Beach Store that has all things necessary for a Gingerbread vacation: beach chairs, oversized towels, and most of all, a wide selection of rain gear. Rain suits, rain boots, rain swimwear.

Last year Annabelle decided she needed a pair of rubber boots. She got these ones with whales printed on them and a matching umbrella, and then danced around the parking lot warbling "Singing in the Rain." I spit up my coffee, staining my shirt, so Annabelle went back in and bought me a bright pink T-shirt that says "Catch Me if You Can, I'm the Gingerbread Man" with a big print of lips on top. Then she dared me to wear it because she knows I can never say no to a dare. Jerk.

When you're with Annabelle, you don't even care that you're wearing the most humiliating shirt ever to come off an assembly line; you actually think it's funny. Not that I'll wear it again anytime soon…

I turn left at the gas station, and then I see it: the boardwalk. I pull into the parking lot where the road ends and the sand of Gingerbread Beach begins. Gingerbread gets so much rain that the sand always has a crispy covering—that's where it gets its name.

When my parents told me they had bought a house here so they could focus on their magazine writing in the summers, I thought they were insane. But as I get out of the car and get my first glimpse of the waves pounding on the shore, see the brightly lit boardwalk (it's lit almost every day because of the weather), and feel the rain on my face, I can't help thinking it was the smartest thing they ever did. That and buying our plasma TV.

I sit on the hood of my car for a few minutes to take it all in and then head over to the boardwalk. I hear the opera before I even get to the door of the Opera Café. I think it's a soprano singing, but it's hard to tell because Jed is belting out the aria along with her. Jed is tone deaf with a voice that sounds like a bullfrog being tortured—it sends the faint of heart running.

The place looks exactly the same: beat-up armchairs and sofas scattered around a dimly lit room that smells like freshly ground coffee and gooey extras like the caramel sauce Annabelle loves to have loaded into her coffee. A couple of summer regulars, Scott Wakeman and Ben Halpert, are playing checkers at a table in the back. Jed keeps a chest of puzzles and games around in case people want to get out of the rain for a while.

"Hey," I say, walking up to the counter.

"Pete!" Jed sets down the dishrag and comes out to slap me on the back. "Did you catch the game last night?"

For fans like us, there is only one team, which means only one game that ever matters. "Yeah," I say. "Those damn Yankees."

Jed laughs. This is his favorite joke because apparently some movie named *Damn Yankees* was made a thousand years ago. I've never seen it, but it has a good name because if there's one thing I hate, it's the New York Yankees who last night blew out my beloved Boston Red Sox.

"We'll get 'em tonight," Jed says, heading back around the other side of the counter. I see that he's lost even more hair over the winter, giving him kind of an owl look. But he's still super-skinny from the running he does on the beach every day before opening the café, which means he gets up at some crazy hour like four.

I like running too, but you'd never catch me up before the sun. For me, the day should start no earlier than ten. But it works for him because Jed's in his late twenties, and he looks fairly good for an old guy. Except for the hair: if I ever start losing mine, I'll just shave it all off.

"We have Beckett pitching," he adds.

I nod. "Just so long as our guys get some hits off Chamberlain."

Jed puts the steaming mug in front of me, and for a moment, I forget everything else as I take a sip.

"I wouldn't mind seeing Theo make a move for somebody before the trade deadline," he says, leaning against the espresso and cappuccino machines. Before I can answer, two dripping-wet tourists come in, and he goes to the register to help them.

"What's up, dude?" Scott asks as he and Ben come up behind me. Ben has the box of checkers; Scott has his palm out, ready for a high five.

"How's it going?" I slap Scott's palm, of course. Scott and Ben are like every other "dude, high five" guy I know. I wonder if around the world, every country has this type of guy who lives for weekend parties, making out with girls he barely knows, and having conversations that never come close to being meaningful. Not that I talk deep philosophy or anything, but after a while, it gets boring to talk about which girl is hottest and who got the drunkest at the last party. Doesn't it?

"Party at the beach tomorrow night, bro," Ben announces with a grin. "We already have the keg lined up."

"Sounds good," I say. I'm not sure if I'll go—it kind of depends how things are with Annabelle—but they're not likely to notice one way or the other. I watch them saunter out. I suddenly feel as if they're my two best friends, even though I can't stand hanging out with them for more than forty-five seconds at a time. They're utterly reliable, I realize. They never, ever change. I haven't seen them in nine months, but it might as well have been nine minutes.

Jed finishes up with the tourists and walks back over to me. "So how was your year?" he asks, giving me a refill. He knows I'll have at least three, so he doesn't bother to ask.

"Pretty good," I say. "I made the varsity team and batted .552." Since baseball season is the best part of school, I start there. I'll finish there, too, since who cares about classes or the endless skiing I had to endure?

Jed raises his eyebrows. "You're full of it," he says.

I can't help grinning a little. "It's not the majors. It's high school."

"Still, five-five-two?" he says, wiping the counter. "I bet I'll be seeing you up at the plate at Fenway one of these days."

Only one person knows what my biggest dream is, and I don't really feel like talking about it now, so I shrug again. "How was the off-season here?"

"Slow," he says. "But hopefully things will pick up now."

Jed pours his whole life into the café. I don't think he ever hangs out with friends or even dates. Annabelle theorizes that he had his heart broken and never got over it, which is why it's just work and baseball.

"So what else do you have for me?" he asks.

I know what he means, but I play dumb. "Not much," I say, trying to think of another topic before he can get started.

"Come on, I want to hear about Gingerbread's greatest romance. How's Annabelle? How's our girl?"

"Well, she's still a Yankees fan," I say, and Jed rolls his eyes. If we can leave it here, it'll be okay.

"It's a curse to be born in New York," he says. "You think *that* is a baseball team when really you're rooting for the Evil Empire."

"Tell me about it."

"You'd think knowing us, she'd see the light," he continued.

"I keep trying." A gust of wind sweeps into the café, bringing with it the briny smell of the sea.

"Did she help you get your fantasy team together this year?" he asks.

"No," I say shortly. This is where I don't want to go.

But Jed is oblivious; why wouldn't he be? "I don't know how she does it. I've never seen anyone who has a sense of baseball like she does."

I take a long swallow of coffee, hoping he'll change the subject.

But he keeps going. "It's like she has this uncanny ability to see how the team will do…she's like some kind of psychic manager." Now Jed is shaking his head in awe of Annabelle's skills.

I used to feel that way too, and beg her for tips. I wonder what Jed would say if he knew the truth about how Annabelle gets her inside scoop.

He looks at me with a lopsided smile. "Maybe she *is* psychic."

I stand up. "I should get going. My folks are going to think I plowed into a truck on I-95 if I don't get over to the house soon."

Just then my cell phone beeps.

"That's probably them now," Jed says.

I nod, even though I know it's not. I have my phone set differently for Annabelle, and this is a text from her. But I'm not telling Jed because who knows what weird stuff she'll have to say.

Jed and I bump fists across the counter while I stare at my phone, and then I head out into the rain. I walk down a few stores and then duck under the awning of Freddy's Fabulous Funnel Cakes and flip open the receiver.

Back home in Gingerbread—hooray! Checked the stars last nite and they are aligned for a great summer. See U soon—A.

I close my phone so hard that it makes a loud snapping sound. The rain drips through my hair and down the back of my neck into my T-shirt. My sneakers get soaked as I walk. I'm not looking where I'm going and stepping in puddles where the planks of the boardwalk gap, but I could care less.

When I get into the car, I turn the key and punch at the radio, then my iPod. *Ahh.* Now I'm surrounded by the pulsing beat of Iggy Pop. Now I can breathe.

She "checked the stars." This is what I don't get. The Annabelle I've known all these years is practical, smart, down to earth. Yes, she can get carried away…but with stuff that's rational, like baseball. Stuff that's in the real world. Not wacky out-there stuff.

Sure, some people are into this sort of thing. There's a group of girls at my school who call themselves a witches' coven and say they practice magic. And Mount Snow has more than one storefront with a psychic. (Four, actually: more psychics than hardware stores in a 100-square-mile area.)

I guess everyone has a pet peeve in life, the one thing that just drives you crazy. For my dad, it's people who don't wax their skis. For my mom, it's anyone who drives over 65 miles per hour. For most Red Sox fans, it's Yankees fans. But freaky New Age types…That's what I don't get. I thought Annabelle didn't get them either.

If the rest of us have to deal with the laws of the universe, the things that suck in the world, and the limits of actual science, well, then why can't they? I mean, these "Wiccan" girls at my school act like they can achieve world peace by boiling eggplant and sage. Come on. If you see a problem, deal with it. Don't act like some stew you call a spell is going to fix anything.

So...

When I first read Annabelle's email confessing her secret about her Red Sox predictions, I assumed she was joking. Because really, how could any sane person take something like astrology seriously for even a second? But she *was* serious. She called me later and started talking about "reading the stars," like stars actually have a message or purpose besides "pumping billions of tons of gaseous fuel into the cosmos." (I'm quoting my science teacher.)

It was unbelievable. I was so appalled that I couldn't say or do anything; I just sat there on my bed listening to Annabelle go on and on about how Jeter had Saturn in his sixth house or something equally insane. Now, four months later, I'm still at a loss for words. Because what can you say when the person you thought you knew best in the world starts talking like a total freak?

And as I gun the motor and skid my way out of the sandy parking lot, I can't help but wonder for the millionth time since she first told me in March...have I ever even known Annabelle at all?

Hillary Lomax

Born April 12: Aries ♈

Rising Sign: Aries ♈

You are focused and determined: when you set your sights on something, those around you had best take cover because you will not stop until you get it. Strong willed and stubborn, you do not always like surprises. But beware this summer: surprises await you, and not all of them are good.

chapter 2

"Annabelle, we're going out to the grocery store," my mom calls up the stairs. "What kind of cereal do you want?"

"None, just some fruit and yogurt," I call down, trying to sound patient. I hadn't eaten cereal since I was twelve and read an article about how processed foods are bad for you. I'm a Leo, and we are sensitive to disease. So I try to be careful about stuff like that. Obviously I make exceptions for the important things, like foamed lattes from the Opera House Café and cotton candy from the amusement park on the boardwalk. A vice or two makes a girl more interesting.

"Are you sure? No Raisin Bran or anything?" she asks.

Somehow, whenever we're at Gingerbread Beach, my mom forgets I'm almost seventeen and starts treating me like I'm ten. Next she'll be asking if I want her to read *Little Women* to me before I go to sleep tonight.

"No, thanks!" I almost trip over the suitcase that's open on the floor. One of the suitcases, that is…there are four total. Plus a duffel bag and a box of books. We're going to be at Gingerbread for eight weeks, so I packed pretty much everything I own. That cut down on the tough decisions about what to take, though my dad's been making lame jokes about needing a U-Haul. He's a light packer and acts like it's the greatest thing ever, but then he wears the same three pairs of shorts and T-shirts the entire summer, so it's clear who's *really* planning wisely.

"Okay, sweetie, we'll be back soon," my mom says. I hear the door slam behind her as she and my dad head out in the rain. I know I should keep unpacking, since it's going to take a while to get my stuff put away in the two old wooden dressers and tiny closet of my attic bedroom, but focusing on anything is hard while I'm waiting for my phone to ring. Or beep with a text. Or the doorbell to buzz. Really, even skywriting will do.

I sent Pete that text exactly eighteen minutes ago, and I'm going slightly crazy waiting for some kind of response. I know he got it, so why hasn't he answered? We've only waited an entire nine months to be together at Gingerbread again. I know he's here because he texted me this morning that his parents got him up at eight and he was pissed about it. Pete is big on sleeping in till at least ten. But that means he got here forty minutes ago at the latest. Knowing Pete, he stopped at the Opera Café first thing. But why isn't he calling?

I swear, if the CIA used waiting for a phone call as their torture method, they'd have people spilling enemy secrets in no time. Not to make light of international torture:

Vanessa, my second best friend at Gingerbread after Pete, makes certain to remind me it is a "very serious issue." (She reads the *New York Times*, watches CNN, and checks various left-wing blogs religiously, trolling for "very serious issues.") But honestly, I am going to go insane if he doesn't get in touch soon.

I decide to try to focus on the unpacking. I sit down on the worn wooden planks of the floor and open my red suitcase, the one with my beach stuff. Of course, the problem there is that everything inside reminds me of Pete. There's the green bikini, my first-ever bikini, that I wore last summer. I still remember the look in Pete's eyes when he saw me.

Come to think of it, that was pretty much the same look he gave the birthday cake at the resort two towns away that was once featured on the Food Network. We went there to celebrate my sixteenth birthday. To this day, it was the best meal of my life. But maybe that's because it was also the best night of my life. Later, when we were walking on the beach, Pete kissed me for the first time.

I'm not exaggerating when I say I've been waiting for that kiss since I was twelve. And let me just add: it was worth the wait. It was the last day of summer; we were at our favorite spot on the beach; and his hands were so soft on my face, his lips so warm…I'm getting the shivers. But shivers are not what I need right now, not when Pete is not calling and my stuff is everywhere. I flip the suitcase closed and open my box of books. There are a library and bookstore here in Gingerbread, so I didn't need to bring novels. But I did need to bring my astrology collection. I wouldn't go away for a weekend without it.

Some people get into astrology to tell their future or navigate romance. And not that I haven't used it for those things too, but the reason I got into it was baseball. I've been a Yankees fan since before I could talk, thanks to my big brother, Gabe, and my Grandma Hillary. Grandma Hillary had us both in Yankees onesies the day we were born. By the time I could talk, Gabe, who was six, was already going to games every season and talking stats.

Grandma Hillary has two loves in her life, baseball and the beach, and she hasn't let anything get in the way of them—not a sun allergy (that was why she bought the house in Gingerbread: lots of rain means very little sun) and not the fact that we live more than five hours from Yankee Stadium. (She has the train schedule from Albany to New York City memorized.) And as Grandma Hillary always says, sports are best served with a big side of trash talk. Even though Gabe and I root for the same team, we find plenty to trash talk about, mainly our fantasy baseball teams.

Fantasy baseball is where you put together a roster of players from a bunch of different teams, and the fantasy team that wins the most games wins the league. That can mean money if you gamble online, which Gabe and I both do. (Yes, it's illegal until we're eighteen, but as I've said, a vice or two makes a girl more interesting.)

More importantly, though, you win bragging rights, which in my house means a lot. And every year, Gabe was the one winning them. But two years ago, I read a blog about assembling a fantasy team and someone mentioned using astrology. I checked my first astrology book out of the library the next day. Halfway through, I was hooked.

Astrology will tell you everything you need to know about a person, all his or her little tendencies and personality traits. From that, you can gauge almost anything: all of life's possibilities—and most important for me, all of baseball's possibilities. That year, I not only beat Gabe, but I swept our entire online league and won a thousand dollars. Not bad for a few hours' work consulting the stars.

After that, I started using astrology for everything: figuring out the best time to prepare my tryout for *Grease* (I got Rizzo), who to work with on my semester-long English project (I went with wildcard Hank Sweet, and we got an A), and of course, predicting real-life baseball winners.

I didn't want to tell anyone about it at first. People can be weirdly judgmental about New Age stuff, I admit. But even though it might sound flaky, it's totally not. Astrology is practically a science; that's why it works. It's been used for thousands of years. My belief is that only the really good stuff, like the wheel or fire, can stand the true test of time.

But still, people can be funny about the stars. Even now, the only person who knows is Pete. He kept asking me where I got such great baseball tips, and finally, a few months ago, I told him.

It's been great having him in on it because now I can just be totally honest about how I chose my fantasy team for this year and why I'm taking extra math courses in the fall. (Leos lack innate business sense, and I may want to run a nonprofit or a theater company one day.) That's the thing about Pete: we tell each other everything, and it was a relief to come clean.

Or so I thought.

Pete. Yet again, everything comes back to him.

Twenty-three minutes and counting...What is going on? Did he forget his cell phone at home? Did he get caught in bad traffic or get a flat? Is he trapped under fallen debris with no access to a communication device? I twist a curl that's fallen out of my ponytail and sigh.

The thing is that Pete isn't just any guy; he's *the* guy. I think some girls (read: me) only really fall in love once. We fall for the guy we are meant for, the one who was in the stars for us since the day we were born. Pete and I were meant to be. It was written in the stars. I mean that literally since I did both our star charts. Well, it took a little tweaking since Leos and Scorpios aren't necessarily the best match. But, yes, once I took into account birth times and rising signs, it was clear: Pete and I were soul mates. And this was our summer to finally be together.

At least it would be if he'd pick up his phone and call me already.

I glare at my cell and then, suddenly, it rings. I'm so surprised I jump. Good thing there's no video. But as I pick up the phone, my heart falls and my eyes prickle a little, which is the weird thing that always happens to me when I'm disappointed. Because it isn't Pete at all; it's Vanessa.

"Hey," I say, trying to sound cheerful. It's not Vanessa's fault she isn't Pete.

"You were hoping it was Pete," she says immediately, without even a "hi."

"Well, kind of." No point in lying since she's already seen right through me. "But I'm happy to hear from you too." That's true too.

"So what, you left him a message and he hasn't called back?" Vanessa asks knowingly.

"No, I haven't called," I say, flopping down on my bed. A text is not a call, so technically I'm being honest.

"A text?"

Okay, this is the thing about Vanessa. We both live in New York State, but she lives in Brooklyn, which is six hours from where I live in Albany (or as she often reminds me, *suburban* Albany)—and we only hang out during the summer, but somehow she can read my mind like *she's* the astrology expert.

"Well, yes, but maybe he's busy driving or dealing with his parents," I say, cringing at how defensive I sound. Vanessa's biggest flaw is that she's a total cynic about guys.

She hasn't always been that way. When I first met her three summers ago, she was as bubbly about guys as all the rest of my friends. But then last summer her boyfriend, Silas, dumped her at the top of the Ferris wheel for this bitchy college girl, Risa. Silas and Risa walked around making out all over the place, and Vanessa has been a "bitter shrew" about guys ever since. Her words, not mine.

"Right," Vanessa says. "Keep telling yourself that. Or just accept wisdom from the bitter shrew herself, that all guys are self-centered jerks, and move on."

"Thanks for the totally unbiased advice," I say, leaning back against the pillows on my bed. They're just the tiniest bit damp from the rain, like everything in Gingerbread, and they smell like the salty sea air, my favorite smell in the world.

She laughs. "You suburban girls live in the land of make believe."

"Right, we don't get reality like you hardened city girls."

"Exactly," Vanessa says. "But seriously, you said he's been acting funny since the spring."

For the millionth time, I curse myself for telling Vanessa that Pete started to change, just a little. The worst thing about it is that I still can't figure out why.

Everything seemed perfect: we were texting and emailing every day, talking for hours every weekend. I turned down almost every guy who asked me out because it was more fun to lie in bed in my pj's and talk to Pete until we were both falling sleep. No way could I go out with some second-rate loser who would talk about himself all night and then paw me at the door when he dropped me off.

But then in March the texts and emails stopped, and Pete was getting off the phone after only five minutes. A few times, he didn't even pick up. And I can't figure out what I did. I mean, it's not like I'm a supermodel or the most fascinating person to talk to. I can't start talk about the latest issues with the Chinese government or whatever, like Vanessa—but the thing is that with Pete, none of that had ever mattered.

He was interested in everything I had to say, even when I was just complaining about first-period gym or how my English teacher is the most sadistic person to live since Charles Manson. I figured it was no big deal until the night before the first Red Sox–Yankees game of the season.

Pete is from New England. The result: he roots for the team of evil, the Boston Red Sox. I am lucky enough to be from the state with the best baseball team in the history of the game, the one that stands for all that is true and good in the world, the New York Yankees. And whenever a Yankees fan and Red Sox fan talk baseball, it gets pretty heated. With me and Pete it can get downright explosive, but there's nothing like some hardcore trash talking to make the games even more awesome.

But that night, when I started riding him about how his team was going down, which would normally make him go off for fifteen minutes, I got a quick, "Whatever. I've got to go." That was when I knew for sure that something was off.

Rather than think too much about what it was, I decided to wait until we were both here, at Gingerbread. Face to face in the place we both love, it would all fall into place again. But then, in a moment of weakness, I spilled the whole thing to Vanessa, and now I have to hear about how Pete is just a schmuck (a Grandma Hillary word) like every other guy. Which is pretty much the last thing you need when you are trying to convince yourself that you've found your soul mate.

"Grandma Hillary and Gabe left last night," I say in a glaringly obvious attempt to change the subject.

Grandma Hillary gave Gabe a two-month trip for his college graduation gift and then decided to tag along with him. They are going to take trains all over Central Asia and Europe. The whole thing would make me beyond jealous if Grandma Hillary hadn't promised me a trip to Greece when I graduate from high school. I've always wanted to see the Acropolis and the places where the Greeks did their stargazing. The ancient Greeks were some of the earliest (and best) astrologers.

"It'll be strange without them here this summer," Vanessa says, sounding like herself and not the bitter shrew.

"I know," I say, feeling the words cut into me. It's the first summer we won't all be together watching Yankees games and going clamming in the rain, Pete and Grandma Hillary trading barbs about baseball. It's just me and my parents—who don't even *like* the Yankees. Though on the bright side, that will mean more time for me and Pete to be alone together…if that's what he wants.

"I think you and I should declare this a guy-free summer," Vanessa announces. "Who needs them? We can read feminist literature and learn Italian and not worry about makeup or styling our hair or any of that crap we do for guys."

I am silent. I like feminist literature as much as the next free-thinking girl, and Italy has pasta and gelato, so who wouldn't want to learn Italian? But she lost me right at the start, with the guy-free summer part.

"What do you say, Annabelle?" she goes on. "Why put yourself through a summer of torture, waiting for Pete to call?"

She's right. Why am I starting to approach this summer like a summer of torture? It doesn't have to be like this at all.

"Vanessa, I have to go," I say, jumping off my bed and stuffing my feet into my blue flip-flops.

"I'll take that as a no," she says, sighing.

"I'll catch up with you later, I promise." I flip my phone closed before she can protest. But I'm on her side: I'm through sitting around waiting for my phone to ring. I don't have time for stupid stuff like that. If I want to talk to Pete, I will just go over to his house and talk to him.

I run down the stairs, grab my whale umbrella, and sprint three houses down to the blue-and-white clapboard house with the Subaru Outback and the silver Honda parked in front. I don't worry about what I will say or how I look. This is Pete. Those things don't matter. What matters is that we are finally going to be together.

I am smiling as I ring the bell. Moments later, the door opens and it's him.

My breath gets lost somewhere down in my chest because I had forgotten how truly gorgeous he is. That thick black hair, those blue eyes, that soft face with the high cheekbones and the little scar on his forehead from the time he tripped over his dad's skis. And those shoulders—those are new!

He's been working out for baseball, and he looks even better than he did last summer…better than how I've pictured him every day since Labor Day. I can even forgive the white Red Sox shirt (puke). The absolute best part is the look in his eyes as he stares back at me, taking me in.

For a second I do wish I had put my caramel curls in a style nicer than a ponytail or put on something besides cutoffs and an old black tank top. But then it doesn't matter because Pete is laughing and he's hugging me and I'm hugging him and everything is just right.

"Hey, you," he says, his mouth so close to my ear I feel his breath. There they are, the shivers again. How did I go so long without this, without him?

"What's up?" I say as he lets me go. "How was your trip?"

"The usual. High-speed chases and international intrigue."

"Meaning you managed to ditch your parents so they couldn't tail you all the way here?" I ask, giddy as he leads me into the living room with its comfortable denim sofa and love seat and the photos of the Alps and magazine covers of stories his parents have written decorating the walls.

He laughs. "Exactly."

We settle on the love seat next to the fireplace that he has going. It crackles and spits, the wood damp even though it was stored inside. He reaches for my hand, and for a moment, his skin on mine feels so good that I can't even speak.

"You guys get here okay?"

"Yes," I say, gulping a little. "Though my dad gave me a hard time about how much I brought. He actually wanted me to leave my astrology books at home." I shake my head in that dads-so-don't-get-it way, but instead of sympathizing, Pete drops my hand and hunches forward, looking into the fire.

"Crazy, right?" I push.

He shakes his head but doesn't say anything.

"I mean, I'm still considering a trade or two for my fantasy team, and I need the stars for that," I say. Baseball will get him talking.

But he just grimaces, like I asked him how to do a calculus problem. Or worse, to root for the Yankees.

"Did you know Beckett has Saturn in his sixth house right now? That's why all the right-handed batters are going to get a bunch of hits off him tonight—"

"Annabelle!" Pete turns and glares—actually *glares*—at me. "Whatever," he says shortly. "Forget it."

I feel like he slapped me. What is going on? Why is he suddenly acting like I brought swine flu over in a cup and offered it to him?

"Upset your guys are going to lose?" I ask, trying to keep my tone light. "Because you will. Chamberlain has Jupiter—"

"Enough with the stupid astrology already!" Pete snaps. "Can't you talk like a normal human being anymore? *I don't care* about Jupiter."

I open my mouth, shocked, but my voice catches in my throat. Before I can ask or say anything else, the back door opens, and in walk Pete's parents. For some absurd reason, each is wearing what appears to be a grown-up sized orange snowsuit, bulky and puffy as the pink one I had when I was eight.

"Annabelle! Wonderful you're here; we need your fashion advice," Pete's mom says as she staggers toward me, sweat beads shining on her face. "This is the latest outfit from Comfortable Ski Wear. It *is* comfortable, but I'm not sure it's fashionable, and my article is on fashion on the slopes. What do you think?"

I'm still so upset by Pete's weirdness that I can only shake my head, and she sighs as she hugs me.

"Just as I feared," she said. "I look ridiculous." She turns to Pete. "What about you, honey? Would you pretend you didn't know me if I showed up wearing this at the next parent-student ski day?'

Usually Pete's mom cracks us both up, but I am closer to crying than laughing.

Pete just shrugs and says again, "Whatever."

"I'm making grilled cheese," Pete's dad says. "I assume you're staying, Annabelle?"

I take a quick look at Pete's face, which is devoid of expression.

"Thanks, but I have to get back," I say, hopping up and shambling toward the front door. I can't even bring myself to look back at the love seat.

"Well, we'll see you soon," Pete's mom calls as I let myself out.

I wait for a moment to see if he'll come after me. He doesn't. He's suddenly more distant than Grandma Hillary and Gabe, who are an entire continent away. I have no idea why, and more importantly, no idea how to bring him back.

Scott Wakeman

Born June 30: Cancer ♋

Rising Sign: Gemini ♊

You are sensitive and self-sacrificing, eager to help out that friend with a broken heart. When it comes to love in your own life, you are the master of mixed messages. But this summer, do what you can to stay honest, because unexpected changes will make things rocky.

chapter 3

I sit on our sun porch and watch dribbles of rain slide down the glass windows overlooking the gray ocean. The tide is coming in, and the waves crash as though they have a beef to settle with the shore. We've had two days of rain at Gingerbread so far, so things are at least off to a good start in one way: practically zero tourists. It's weird how fast I've already gotten into a routine: working out in the mornings, getting coffee at the Opera Café, hanging out at home going through the practice SAT test book my parents got for me. Maybe I can get used to being alone.

My SAT scores were fine when I took the test last year, but my parents figure one more shot at perfection won't hurt, especially since I'm mostly just taking it easy this summer. I'll try to find a job at some point. But as Annabelle says, people who can afford to ski can afford to tip. And the guests at the lodge where I work part-time during the winter are great tippers. I don't really need the money…I don't even know what I'd spend it on…

What I haven't been doing is thinking about Annabelle. At all. Well, except for just now, or to wonder why she hasn't called or texted. I mean, okay, I guess I know: she's pissed about how I clammed up when she came over. She hates stony silences more than anything. It's not like I meant to do it, but what could I say? Jeter has the moon in his garage, or whatever? Give me a break. This is why I haven't been thinking about her.

I get up to grab a glass of water and try to figure out what to do for the rest of the day. I already went running. Jed was busy with a big crowd of senior citizens in for a bingo tournament at the rec hall this afternoon, so I didn't hang out long at the Opera Café. It's too early for lunch, and I'm not really in the mood to do more stupid multiple-choice practice questions.

If I'm honest, I have to admit that I really only want to do one thing: hang out with Annabelle. Gingerbread isn't Gingerbread unless I'm hanging out with Annabelle. For the zillionth time, I think about how good she looked when she came over, her caramel curls falling out of her ponytail onto her face, her eyes all lit up and excited.

All right, all right; I *have* been thinking about her.

My mom has always says Annabelle has "a true zest for life," which is a painfully dorky way to put it (though not as dorky as her orange snowsuit), but it's true. Annabelle gets so into things you can't help getting into them too.

Except...I just can't go along for the ride with this astrology junk. But maybe if I don't respond, she'll just let it go and we can talk about other stuff, normal stuff, like baseball and school and who is going to cream who at mini-golf.

Screw it. I can't wait any longer.

Yes, part of me is still worried Annabelle has changed or was hiding a freak side this whole time, but I'm picking up my phone and texting before I think about it too much.

Meet me @ the beach in 15?

A walk in the rain is one of our usual summer rituals. Walking in the rain may not sound fun to most people, but Annabelle could make rummaging through a garbage dump a blast. Besides, it takes a certain special kind of person to appreciate a rainy beach. The sand is packed down tight so it's easy to walk, and we always have the whole place to ourselves—just the waves, the sky, the sand, and us. Honestly, it might be my favorite way to spend time outside of Fenway Park.

I know she'll show, so I don't bother waiting for her reply. I just put on my beat-up sneakers and old navy raincoat and head out. I jog over to our spot: a little dune almost exactly halfway between our two houses. The rain is a light mist, so I take off the jacket and toss it on the sand. For a moment, I just watch the rain hit the churning ocean, tiny droplets disappearing into the gray-green water.

"Forgot your skis?" I hear behind me.

I turn, unable to hide my smile. She's got on her green army shorts and a pink camisole. Corny? I don't care: I swear the sight of her makes my heart stop for a second. Her hair is back in a headband, flying free behind her, and her eyes are sparkling. She walks right up and punches me on the arm. I'd forgotten how strong she is, and I yelp before I can stop myself.

She laughs. "Uh-oh. You're not getting soft on me, are you?"

"That's so weird…I just had the funniest sensation I was bit by a mosquito…"

"Macho is worse than soft," she says.

"I don't care," I say, wrapping an arm around her. "I'm all guy all the time."

"I wish I had a tape recorder to broadcast that across the boardwalk. Just to clarify: that wasn't you tearing up last summer when we watched *The Notebook* at my house?" She leans into me, and for a second, all I do is inhale the mix of her rose shampoo, fresh coffee, and the smell that is just her, Annabelle.

"I was crying from boredom." Yes, I am a total sucker for tearjerker movies, but I've never actually admitted it out loud. Yes, with Annabelle, there's no need.

"Yeah, keep telling yourself that. Just like you're going to keep telling yourself the Sox are going to win the division, and this is the year you're going to beat me in fantasy baseball."

I'm definitely not going there. Instead I take her hand, and we start walking down the beach. Just touching her hand makes my whole body feel alive and awake. I've been holding hands with girls since I was thirteen. But that's the thing: I've been holding hands with "girls." They might as well all be the same. When I hold hands with Annabelle, I'm holding hands with a...person.

Did I say I'm a sucker for tearjerker movies? *Just please, please don't bring up astrology,* I silently beg.

"So how are your brother and grandma doing?" I ask. That's a safe topic.

"I just heard from Gabe last night," she says, her steps falling naturally in sync with mine. "He said they're in Kazakhstan and they ate horse."

"Horse, as in..."

"As in what cowboys ride. No one should eat the Black Stallion."

I laugh, even though I'm grossed out. "I am with you on that one. Jeez. This will sound bad...but how did it taste?"

"He said it was pretty good actually, but you know Gabe. He'll eat anything."

I remember last summer when he ate two bags of clams from Moe's, the greasiest, oldest seafood in Gingerbread and possibly in the world. "Good point."

"He also told me that if I use his computer while he's gone, he'll make my senior year a living hell."

"That was the best he could come up with? A living hell? That's not so bad."

"He doesn't have a whole lot going on upstairs," she says. "Maybe the trip will do him some good. Grandma says he's a late bloomer."

A gull flies low over the water and then ducks in after a fish.

"Some things never change," I say. "Like Gabe's brain."

"Which, at times, can be a good thing."

"Or the worst thing ever."

She laughs. "Your parents seemed happy yesterday."

"Can we not talk about it?" I say, rolling my eyes. Obviously Annabelle has seen my parents at their worst, but it's still less than ideal to have them walking around in some of the gear they test out. Yesterday wasn't that bad, but my mom mentioned that her next article is on a new line of "sexy skiwear" (her words) for teens, which should be mortifying. Especially if she shows up wearing it at the Opera Café—which she's been known to do, claiming she needs to get reactions from a crowd. "I think it's going to get worse. They looked like giant traffic cones."

"Well, as long as there's no lederhosen involved," she says.

I laugh. A little too loudly. Two years ago my dad posed for an Austrian magazine article on "ski instructors over fifty," and they had him in lederhosen. Any normal person would do all he could to bury this, but my dad is actually proud of it. He had the picture framed.

"Is he still looking for the picture?" she asks, grinning.

"It was the first thing he mentioned when we got to the house. He was sure it was here somewhere, and he said he had to find it before the summer was over."

"Good luck to him on that," she says.

We both laugh. Last summer, I took the picture down when I was having one of those my-parents-aren't-home parties, and Annabelle said she'd help me make it disappear for good. She has it hanging up in her closet in Albany.

"Just be careful he doesn't learn how to download a copy of it."

I think of my dad swearing as he tries to log into his email without my mom's help. "No worries there. Plus he really liked that it was the original cover. He wouldn't be as psyched about a copy."

"Yeah, it was a true classic," Annabelle says. "I keep hoping they'll do a follow-up cover story on ski instructors and their kids—and get *you* into some lederhosen."

"Does that mean I'd have to learn German?"

She laughs, squeezing my hand tightly. "Come on, you'd look cute in the shorts. Maybe they could even get a shot with one of those mountain goats. Oh, wait: I forgot your fear of farm animals."

Now she's crossed a line. Annabelle claims to not be ticklish, but I know better. I get her right in the soft part of her belly, and she doubles over, shrieking with laughter.

"Enough! Enough!" she wails, each word punctuated with giggles.

"What was that you said?" I asked, tickling harder.

"That you are…brave and manly…even in the face of life-threatening pigs," she chokes out, shrieking.

A few years ago, we went with Grandma Hillary to a farm stand about an hour away. We wandered around while Grandma Hillary shopped for produce, and we ended up finding this massive pigpen. Annabelle dared me to run in and touch the pig trough. It didn't seem like that big a deal because all the pigs were hanging out in the mud sleeping. But I guess they thought I was going to feed them, because I was mobbed. Those things can hustle when they want to. And they are big. Annabelle will never let me forget how fast I got out of there.

"I didn't hear you," I say, ticking harder.

"You are…fearless and masculine…in the face of great danger!" she shouts. "Arghhh! *Stop it!*"

I let go of her and she leans against me, giggling one last time and sighing. "Masculine and very fast."

She links her arm with mine and her skin feels soft, once again making it hard to think. "So did you survive the end of ski season?" she asks, actual sympathy in her voice. Not that it's the kind of tragedy that deserves a telethon or anything, but it sucks to be the only person in my town who hates skiing. Especially since my parents are the biggest ski advocates out there.

I shrug. "It's over, so that's good."

"I don't know who thought going down a mountain on two planks was worth anyone's time," she says. "It seems like cheating. Real athletes run."

"Tell that to Coach. He acted like I was violating some Law of the Universe when I refused to go on the ski weekend he set up for the team. He said he did it *because* of me."

"What does *he* know?" she asks indignantly. "What if you got injured and couldn't play this season? You're going after a baseball scholarship and getting interest from team scouts. Like you'd risk all of that for some stupid male-bonding-down-a-mountain trip? Just because your parents are instructors? What a moron."

I swear: if I were dying of bubonic plague with boils all over me, Annabelle could make me feel better about it.

"I bet that guy is a Capricorn," she adds.

Oh, no...

But she doesn't seem to notice as I stiffen next to her. "They can be the type to only see their own agenda."

Please, no...

"Yeah, well, that's Coach," I say weakly, fighting to get things back on track. "It's his way or the highway."

She nods knowingly. "Yup. A total Capricorn. But you're a Scorpio, so you can handle him."

I detach my arm from hers and put a few inches between us as she starts going into traits of a Capricorn.

"The fact that you're stubborn works for you here," she concludes, looking at me with a completely serious smile, as if I'm supposed to be grateful for the "facts" she's spewing. As if something so insane jibes with everything else about her: her humor, her intelligence, her...everything.

I say nothing and just keep walking.

"I know, you're thinking that you'll butt heads," she adds.

I look her in the eye. "You're right. I am thinking that. And it doesn't—"

"Trust me: he's going to back down if you handle him right. Capricorns can be made to see reason if you present things in a way they can hear."

Interesting. Now she's talking about reason, as if there's anything reasonable about looking at the sky for answers on how to handle an ornery coach.

"Will you give it a try?" she persists.

"Um, I don't think advice from the stars is what I need here," I finally mumble. "Really it's not even a problem. It was just one ski trip."

I realize I'm speeding up and Annabelle has to trot a little to keep up with me. Normally I try to be considerate about the fact that her legs are a lot shorter than mine, but now I just want to get back home.

Annabelle frowns. "Pete, wait—"

"I just want to get home, okay? You reminded me...I need to study for the SATs." I debate whether I should say anything about how I think she's gone off the deep end with this star stuff, but before I can think of a way to put it, she crosses her arms over her chest and glares at me.

"I don't get you," she says. "I'm just trying to help."

By talking like a crazy person?

"I've got to get going," I say, trying not to think about how beautiful she looks in the rain and the wind.

"Pete!" she yells as I practically sprint off the beach toward home. "You forgot your jacket..."

But I'm going at a full clip now, and there's no way I'd turn back, even if she had every stitch of clothing I owned plus my lucky mitt. Nothing could convince me to go back to that conversation about the stars. I'm just heading upstairs, plugging into *Never Mind the Bollocks; Here's the Sex Pistols*—and tuning out everything that's happened in the last hour.

Ben Halpert

Born January 5: Capricorn ♑

Rising Sign: Gemini ♊

You are well organized, but your suitors had best proceed with caution because under that aggressive shell lies one cool customer. Those close to you are in on your secret: they know your soft side and the kindness you can show when you care. This summer, it is your pride you have to watch out for and your ambition that you will need because it is a long road to reach your true goal.

chapter 4

"See you guys later," I call to my parents as I open the front door and step out into another morning's drizzle. My dad is tucked away in his study working. Being a computer programmer has its perks: his company lets him work from home over the summer. On the other hand, my mom, who teaches preschool, has nothing but time on her hands. She waves from the kitchen where she's trying to make gazpacho. Cold tomato soup. If there were ever a perfect dish for a perfectly miserable day…

"Have a great time, honey! Love you!"

"Thanks," I mutter. Her send-off is a little over the top considering I'm going for a cup of coffee, but she's at loose ends this summer with Grandma Hillary and Gabe gone. That or she sensed that my trip to the Opera Café is not just an innocent quest for good coffee but in fact a mission to save my entire summer. Because it's been three days since Pete left me stranded on the beach for no reason…three long days when I've broken down every piece of dialogue, every scrap of physical contact—trying to figure out what made him change from sweet, wonderful Pete into grumpy, silent Pete.

It can't just be the astrology, can it?

Vanessa says it's just typical jerk behavior. Since all guys are jerks, I shouldn't be surprised. But Pete is not a jerk. I know this. At least I think I do.

At least I know Pete gets coffee after his morning jog on the beach around eleven. I will be getting there right after he takes that first sip.

The rain starts falling a little harder, and I put up my whale umbrella to protect my hair. I styled it back in a twist that makes my face look slim (at least I read somewhere it does), but I can feel curls leaking out already. I'm wearing my white lace halter top, the one Pete couldn't take his eyes off last summer, and a short pink skirt. I put on real shoes, my black ballet flats, instead of flip-flops. Not that Pete cares so much about clothes, but when you're on a mission, you give it everything you've got. I even put on a little makeup.

I hear Jed belting out an aria as I walk into the Opera Café. He's at the cappuccino machine, tending to a long line of customers. My heart pounds for a moment. Pete is sitting at the counter, nursing a white ceramic mug filled with the house blend. Why he keeps his coffee plain is beyond me. It should be foamy milk, sweet cinnamon, zesty peppermint, or gooey caramel. Coffee, like most things in life, should be fun. *Right, Pete?* I want to yell at him. *Aren't I right?*

If I keep my eyes off the little Red Sox insignia on his jersey, he looks perfect.

Scott and Ben move up next to him as they wait for their coffee.

"Hey," I say, walking up to them.

"Hey, sexy," Scott says, without a trace of irony.

"Looking good, Annabelle," Ben adds, smirking a little.

This is how the Gingerbread Beach boys (and most boys, come to think of it) talk to all breathing females, but it still feels good. Admiration is admiration, after all. Pete finally turns and offers a smile.

"What's up?" I say, trying to sit gracefully on the stool next to him but somehow losing my shoe as I settle.

"You lost your shoe," Pete says, chuckling.

"Yes, I know. I planned it that way." I shake off the other one, trying to look like I want to be barefoot on a cold, rainy day—in a café that is not swept *nearly* as much as it could be. We Leos can be neat freaks.

"Trying to drive out the customers with a little foot odor?" Pete jokes.

I try to raise an eyebrow but end up laughing.

"What can I get you, love?" Jed asks, bustling over. He has coffee stains on his white apron, and he smells like beans.

"How about a gingerbread latte?" I ask.

"Touristy," Pete tells me as Jed goes over to the coffee machine.

"Classic," I correct.

"Speaking of which, you guys missed a classic party the other night," Scott says, leaning his elbows on the counter.

Jed sets my drink down, and I pick up the mug, losing myself in the scent for a moment.

"Carl got so wasted he started imitating Jed singing opera," Scott adds. "Jen recorded him on her phone and put it up on YouTube. You should totally check it out."

"Absolutely: I wouldn't want to miss that," Pete says, sounding very serious.

"Me neither," I agree. "It sounds...*epic*."

Pete pokes me in the side. Scott and Ben don't notice because they are busy checking out the girl who just walked in.

"Talk about hot," Scott says in his most sleazy voice.

"I'm loving that skirt," Ben agrees.

I look over at the girl in question. "Skirt" is too generous a description for the scrap of leather around her hips. She'd better be careful if she wants to sit down in that thing. She has a tattoo on her bicep and another on the back of her neck. Her dirty-blond hair is up in a sloppy knot on top of her head so you get full view of the rose complete with thorns etched just below her hairline.

Scott shifts on his stool to get a better view of Tattoo Girl. His arm bumps Pete's coffee.

"Whoops! Sorry, dude," Scott says, reaching for a napkin. The coffee is all over Pete's hands; a little has splashed onto his jersey.

"No problem," Pete says, standing up. "I'll just go rinse this out..."

"While you're at it, I think you should toss the whole thing," I whisper.

Pete snickers as he heads back to the bathroom.

I take a sip of my latte, which is buttery smooth and rich, but then I almost choke when Tattoo Girl comes over and sits on Pete's stool. I start to tell her that seat is taken, which should be obvious since there's a mug of coffee sitting there and she witnessed the spillage, but she turns her back to me.

"Sarah," she says, reaching out to shake Scott's hand.

He practically purrs. "Scott, and it's a true pleasure."

I can't see Sarah's face, but I imagine a smug look of satisfaction. I roll my eyes. I hate it when a girl ignores all fellow females in the vicinity. It doesn't help that Scott and Ben are falling all over her like she's some kind of goddess. Sure, she's pretty (in a B-level, MTV-extra sort of way), but is that any reason to fawn all over her and completely forget that I exist? I mean, we were talking.

"We're having a party Saturday night," Ben tells Sarah. "We have a keg lined up, and it's going to be pretty wild."

Okay, obviously yes: it is enough for him to completely forget I exist because he doesn't even include me in the party invite. Not that I am much for a "wild" time like Sarah with her tattoos obviously is, but Ben has known me since we were twelve. I have distinct memories of saving him from the wrath of Laser Tag Larry, in fact: memories which I'm sure would embarrass the hell out of him. You'd think Ben would at least look my way when talking about a party.

"Good as new," Pete says as he comes up, a huge wet spot on his jersey but all the coffee rinsed away. He reaches over, grabs his mug off the counter, and drains the last of it.

Sarah turns, her eyes suddenly bright with interest.

"How rude! I took your seat," she says in a low voice that she clearly thinks is sexy. Really it just sounds like she has a sore throat. "I'm Sarah."

"Hey," Pete says, wiping his arm across his mouth.

"Are you here for the summer or just passing through?" she asks, leaning toward him. Scott and Ben are forgotten, and not once has she glanced my way. *Spotlight: Pete!* Seriously, it's like he is suddenly the only person in the café. And can you get any cheesier in terms of a come-on? This girl is ridiculous.

"Here for the summer," Pete says.

Sarah smiles. "Me too."

I suddenly feel prissy in my lacy white shirt that had seemed sexy. It makes me look like a nun next to Sarah and her low neckline.

All of a sudden, Pete turns to me and holds out his hand. "Let's go," he says, lacing his fingers through mine.

The anger melts away in an instant. I smile at Sarah. "I'm Annabelle. It's so nice to meet you," I say before I allow Pete to lead me out.

Sarah smiles back and mumbles, "Hey," but her eyes are burning. Ben and Scott resume falling all over her. It's too funny. Besides, who cares about them? I'm leaving with the only guy who really matters. Sarah can have them—and any other guy she wants.

We walk out into the rain, which has quieted back down to a drizzle. Pete is still holding my hand as we start walking up the boardwalk, passing Seashells and Sand Dollars, a tiny boutique that sells jewelry made from stuff on the beach, and the booth where Dan, an ancient artist, will do portraits and caricatures. A kid with a pointy nose is wiggling in the posing chair while his mom tries to hold him still so Dan can sketch him.

"So what have you been up to?" I ask Pete. It feels so natural to have my hand tucked into his, so right.

"Mostly just practicing for the SAT," he says.

My scores were good so I'm not going to be taking the exam again. Thank goodness—I hate standardized tests. Not that anyone in her right mind would like them, but given that I'm a Leo, I don't have the patience for mindless, tedious tasks.

"You know how to live it up," I say, and he laughs.

"What were you up to besides checking out the fall schedule on Broadway?" he teases. He knows me too well.

"One day it might be me starring there," I say.

He squeezes my hand, and the shivers run down my arm. "I'd bet on it," he says in that way that makes me feel like I could do absolutely anything.

"Right, and between shows I'll come see you play ball," I say, and I mean it. "Though I'll be rooting for the Yanks even if it is you batting for Boston."

"You and Grandma Hillary," he says.

I laugh. We pass a group of moms with toddlers who are just out of the bouncy, blow-up tent with balls. You can tell by how the kids' hair is flying every which way and how they are hopping around, as though they're still walking on cushions.

"I miss her," I hear myself say. "They're in Uzbekistan now, on some part of the Silk Road. It sounds amazing."

Pete drops my hand and wraps an arm around my shoulders. "I know she misses you too," he says.

How does he pull this off? How can he go from so jokey to so wonderful in the space of a breath? His words warm every part of me, and I'm all tingly from his arm snug around me. It's like he has a sensor tuned into me and what I'm feeling and then knows exactly what to say. He gets it right every time; that's how I know we were written in the stars.

"So your Yankees went down last night," he says as we pass the arcade. I hear bleeps and shouts coming from inside where the twelve-year-old club is hanging out. I feel a sudden wave of nostalgia.

"It was a fluke," I say airily. "Plus we'll get hot when it counts."

"I hope you don't lose the American League East waiting for that hot streak," he says.

"As a matter of fact, it looks like we're due a serious winning streak in August," I say without thinking.

Pete's arm falls off my shoulders, and his face is suddenly set in that distant mask that is starting to become alarmingly familiar. But I'm not doing this again. I didn't mention astrology; isn't that enough?

"What?" I ask.

He shrugs and then turns to look at the amusement park set up at the end of the boardwalk. I see him looking at the Ferris wheel where Silas dumped Vanessa last year.

"Pete, we have to talk. No running off saying you have something urgent at home. I want to know what's going on with you. Just *tell* me, okay?"

He looks at the ocean, scuffs his sneaker on a loose board, and then rubs his face. I'm going to scream if he doesn't start using actual words, but finally he opens his mouth. "It's just the astrology stuff," he says, avoiding eye contact.

"That's it?" I ask, confused. That can't be the *entire* reason he's been acting so aloof the past few months, why he suddenly turns on and off—can it?

"I'm just not into it," he says.

"That's fine, though I bet if I told you more about it, you might be," I say, trying not to sound too eager. "Like did I tell you how I used it to win the Super Bowl pool in my drama club and I don't even watch football?"

"Yeah, you mentioned it like ten times," he says in a flat voice.

"Okay, whatever...I was excited!" I exclaim, even though I'm sulking inside. *Like you don't repeat things you care about,* I add bitterly, in silence.

"Just...you can keep it to yourself, right?" he asks awkwardly.

"Wait, what? Are you telling me I can't talk about astrology with you at all?" Bitterness morphs to outrage. I'd listen to him talk about anything he wants. *Anything.* Last year, he went on for hours about his athlete's foot—and did I complain or tell him to stop, even when it got really gross? No, I did not.

"Pretty much, yeah—at all," he says, finally looking at me. "It's weird...Don't you see that?"

I don't like anything about what he's just said to me. "It's not weird," I say coldly. "It's an ancient science that has been around for centuries. Lots of brilliant people have used it, like Newton and Pythagoras."

"So maybe they were freaks in their spare time?" he asks in that familiar jokey voice he uses to talk about people like Laser Tag Larry, people who are so odd that they defy explanation—a voice that almost always makes me laugh.

"Are you saying I'm a freak?" I demand.

He lets out a loud sigh. Now he sounds like my father. "No, I don't mean it like that. It's just that anyone who would believe that looking up at the sky can tell you something about your life is one card shy of a full deck, you know?"

"No, I do not know!" I am pissed now.

"How can you take that stuff seriously?" His voice is getting louder too. "It's ridiculous to think these things made of gas and energy billions of miles away have anything to do with us."

"So now I'm ridiculous *and* a freak?" I practically shout.

He shrugs again, like it doesn't matter. "I'm just saying what any reasonable person thinks: that stuff is for flakes who can't handle the real world."

I take a deep breath so my voice won't shake when I reply. "Then I guess I won't be bothering you with my *flaky* ideas anymore."

I turn and stalk down the boardwalk, toward the beach and my house. I expect him to follow, to apologize for being a judgmental snob, to say he cares about me so much I can talk about paint drying on walls and he'll listen. But there is no calling of my name, no running to catch up with me. He is letting me go.

Sarah Sheldon

Born November 29: Sagittarius ♐

Rising Sign: Scorpio ♏

You are the life of the party even though you love to flit from one event to the next, seeking excitement and fun above all else. Your enthusiasm for life charms others, though they can be taken aback at your willingness to speak the truth. Generally you like to see people united, but others best beware because this summer you are all about shaking things up—and not for the better.

chapter 5

"Catch you later, dude," Scott says, saluting me as he heads out of the teen pool hall. If "teen pool hall" sounds glamorous, allow me to clarify: it's a tiny, rotting wooden building on the boardwalk with a bunch of pool tables crammed in, a ping-pong table in the back (no one ever plays, because the humidity has warped the surface), and a bar along one side where Margo, the grizzled owner (also warped from constant humidity and who-knows-what), serves supermarket-brand soda for inflated prices. But the pool is cheap, and that's what I'm here for.

Ben waves as he follows Scott out. Night is falling over Gingerbread Beach, and the rain has finally stopped—for now. I just finished beating them both, twice, so they don't invite me to go with them wherever they're going. But I don't care. It's not like I'd go with them anyway. I'm not in the mood for a party or "cruising chicks" (their words) at the Friday night dance at the rec hall.

I only have one girl on my mind, and I doubt she'll be there. I haven't seen her anywhere the past few days, not that

I've been looking. Much. I mean, looking for Annabelle would be stupid since there's really nothing to say. She's changed into a New Age stranger. I haven't. That's that.

I just wish I could stop thinking about her.

I rack the scratched-up colored balls and chalk up my cue. So, this is what my summer has come to: solo pool. It could be worse, I suppose. Not sure how, but…

"Bet you a beer I can take this game," a husky female voice says.

I look up and see the girl from the Opera Café, the one with the tattoos. Today she's wearing a black dress with no back, and I can't help but zero in on a snake tattoo at the base of her spine as she sashays over to grab a cue stick. But sexy tattoo or no, I'm not in the mood for company.

"I'm just messing around," I say when she returns. "Maybe another time."

She smirks at me from behind lowered lashes. She's wearing too much black stuff on her eyes, but underneath it, I have to admit…she really is pretty.

"What, are you scared I'll beat you?" she asks. "I *am* good. Come on…one game. I dare you."

She said the magic words that can get me to do almost anything. I never, ever turn down a dare.

"One game," I say, but I realize she wasn't even waiting for me to agree. She's already pulled up the rack and is lining up her cue to break. I can tell by the smack of the cue ball against the others that she is for real. Good. I'm up for a challenge.

She has four stripes in holes before I know it, and I have to work hard to match that. She smiles like a cat the whole time I'm doing it, her arms folded over her chest.

"Not bad," she tells me. "But this game is mine." She proceeds to pocket the rest of her balls and then shoots me a wicked grin. "Eight in the top left," she says, and moments later the black ball is flying in.

I admit it; I'm impressed.

"You owe me a beer," she says, swinging her cue gently between two fingers.

"Will you settle for a soda?" I ask. "Considering it's all they serve here."

She tilts her head. "Really? I thought there was a secret handshake or something that could get you something more exciting."

I shake my head. "Excitement is definitely not what this place is about..."

"Fine, I'll take it, but you still owe me a proper beer," she says. "I'll have anything diet."

I can't help smiling a little as I head up to the crowded bar and order two colas, one diet.

"Who's the smoking hot babe?" a guy named Walker asks. He's part of the Scott and Ben crowd. He just graduated, and I've heard he's off to Penn State on a football scholarship. Normally he wouldn't bother with a guy like me, younger and not into parties or football, but right now he's leaning forward eagerly.

"Her name is Sarah," I say casually.

We both look over at her, and she blows a kiss right at me. It's so corny I almost cringe, and I feel my cheeks turn red. But Walker is impressed.

"Dude, she is *into* you," he says, with admiration in his voice.

I can't help but feel good. But honestly, it's so over the top that I half-expect Ashton Kutcher to burst in and tell me I've been "punked."

"Yes, she is," a voice laced with hostility says.

I turn and see Vanessa glaring at me. She's wearing a wool sweater, and with her horn-rimmed glasses, she honestly looks about thirty years old—like a vengeful aunt or schoolteacher. Vanessa has always been a girl who deliberately goes out of her way to dress down.

"Where's Annabelle?" she asks loudly.

I shrug and focus on paying the bartender for the sodas. "Not sure," I say.

Walker whistles. "Dude, how many girls are you stringing along this summer?"

"Yes, *Dude*, how many?" Vanessa asks, her voice acid.

Suddenly the pool hall, with its low ceiling and perpetual moisture and crowd, feels claustrophobic. The smell of the old pinewood floor, mixing with the smell of sweat and stale humidity, are making me nauseous. I take a long sip of my cola and then smile flatly at Vanessa.

"I would have to say that I am stringing exactly zero girls along this summer," I respond. I can see Walker laughing behind her, like he's in on the fact that I am suddenly Gingerbread Beach's resident stallion, but now his admiration feels stupid and empty. "I'm just playing some pool," I tell them both.

I grab the sodas and head over to Sarah.

She's still staring at me, her fingers brushing mine as she takes the glass. "Thanks," she says, and takes a sip.

I gulp down my drink and let the ice slide into my mouth, then crunch down on it. I'm feeling very lost at the moment, and I'm not sure why—as if I'm watching somebody else pretending to be me, living in some strange alternate universe that bears no resemblance to the summer beach town I know.

"What kind of soda is this?" she asks, her forehead wrinkled as she holds her glass out like it's got an insect floating in it.

"Margo brews it herself in the Margo-tron," I say automatically. That's the lame inside joke the Gingerbread Beach regulars have been telling since I was twelve years old, as stale and unfunny as the air itself.

But Sarah bursts out laughing. "The way they cut corners really gives it a unique taste," she says, setting the glass down on the floor under our pool table. "Kind of like upholstery cleaner."

"Yeah, that should be Margo's slogan: refresh yourself and clean your sofa, all with one bottle."

She laughs again, a low throaty sound that reminds me of movie stars from the old black-and-white movies my parents like. Maybe she's not so bad, this girl…

"How about another game?" she asks.

"Sure," I say. Why not? She's clearly a pool shark, and the game will take my mind off Vanessa and her judgments. Anyway, what's it to Vanessa if I play pool with another girl? Or if I do anything else? It's not like Annabelle needs a watchdog. And what would Vanessa be watching out for anyway? Annabelle and I have gone completely bust this summer. I'm not going to obsess over it.

Sarah racks up the balls and we play in silence, each of us focusing on our shots. This is how I like it. I don't play that many games, but the ones I play I take very seriously. (Yes, even laser tag.) Scott and Ben were so busy checking out girls they wouldn't notice if they hit the opponent's ball instead of their own. But Sarah is like me. We duke it out to the eight ball, and then I pocket it.

"Nice game," she says.

"Thanks." I lean back against the table, feeling…I don't even know what. Smug? Confident? Weird?

"But next time, I'll kick your butt."

I grin. Bring on the trash talk, I almost say…But then the grin fades.

"I owe you a drink," she says, reaching for her bag.

I glance at the bar. Vanessa is still there. "No, I'm good," I say.

"A rain check then," she says. "For a real one."

"Okay." I'm not much into beer, but I wouldn't mind hanging out with Sarah again. At least she's not into New Age "science." I hope.

"So I see you like my guys," she says, gesturing to my Red Sox jersey.

"You're a Sox fan?" I ask and she nods. Now I'm grinning again. Yet another reason to hang out.

"I catch as many games as I can, but it's hard living in California and all."

"Where in California?"

"San Francisco," she says.

"I've heard it's a great city," I say, trying to sound worldly. I actually heard that from my mom who went there for a weekend when she was doing a teaching stint, but Sarah doesn't have to know that.

She wrinkles her nose. "It's okay, I guess. It gets old after a while. I'm going to NYU this fall, and I can't wait. It's going to be a relief to be in a real city where people really *live*, you know?"

I swallow. A college girl. Or about to be. "I don't know," I say, not letting on that the NYU thing impresses me. "That's Yankees territory."

Sarah grins. "Well, I guess every place has a downside. Though it can't be as bad as here. This rain is going to make me crazy. I feel like I never left the Bay Area. Does it ever stop?"

It's funny. Before this summer, I'd have said Gingerbread has no downside: that it's as close to perfect as a place could be. But now? Even the rain I used to love feels depressing.

"Not really," I say.

Sarah shakes her head. "I can't believe my parents are making us stay the entire summer at a beach where it rains every day. It's insanity."

"At least you won't get a sunburn," I point out.

She smiles slowly, looking right into my eyes. "But I was so looking forward to wearing my new string bikini."

My head glazes over a little because that really does sound pretty great, even though if Annabelle were here, she'd probably make the universal sign for barfing. I try to ignore Vanessa's icy glare across the room. "Well, we do get a few days of sun."

She nods, her smile getting bigger. "I'll look forward to that, then—"

"Pete!" The sharp voice makes me jump.

Speak of the devil... There she is: Annabelle, her eyes flashing, her hands on her hips. I can't help but smile, though, because with her cheeks all flushed and her hair a cloud around her face, she looks completely...herself. But then I focus and see how her mouth is a thin line and how she's shooting an evil glance at Sarah. I'm thinking I can thank Vanessa for Annabelle's sudden appearance, but I'll be annoyed about that later. Right now, I have enough to handle.

"What's up?" I say calmly, like I think everything's fine.

"Can I speak to you for a moment?" she hisses. "In private?"

Sarah moves closer to me.

"Sure," I say. I turn to Sarah. "See you later."

Sarah stares straight at Annabelle as she answers. "You can count on it. Remember, you still owe me a beer."

Nice, I think, feeling slightly sick. Annabelle is going to have a field day with that one. I grab my jacket off the folding chair and follow Annabelle outside, where, of course, it's raining again: heavy droplets that slip down my face as I walk. The tide must be going out because the waves are soft as they hit the beach in the cool night air.

Annabelle leads me down the boardwalk without speaking and stops at some benches that face the water. But instead of sitting, she leans back against one, brushes her wet hair back from her face, and stares me down.

"What are you doing?" she demands.

"Playing pool."

"You know that's not what I mean," she says.

I'm starting to get annoyed. "I'm not sure I do."

"What are you doing with *her*?" Annabelle says in exasperation.

"Playing pool," I say again. I can tell by the way she squeezes her eyes shut for a moment that she is as annoyed as I am. But what does she want from me? She asked what I was doing, and I told her. Can't she see that *she's* the problem?

"That girl is trouble," Annabelle says. She pulls away from the bench and begins to pace a little, her flip-flops splashing on the wet surface.

I have to laugh. "How do *you* know? You've never even spoken to her."

"I don't have to speak to her to see the obvious," she says.

"What, you're judging her based on a couple of tattoos and a tight dress?"

Oops. I probably shouldn't have mentioned that the dress was tight.

"No, I'm not judging her," Annabelle snaps. "But things like that tell you about a person. The way you present yourself speaks volumes about what's inside. And she wants to buy you a beer!"

"Is that part of your astrology wisdom?" I ask, ignoring the beer part since it's not a big deal. "Or something you got out of a fortune cookie?"

Annabelle throws up her arms. "I can't say anything to you anymore without you making some kind of snotty remark! If anyone here has a problem being judgmental, it's you."

"What am *I* judgmental about?" I ask. "I'm the one who's being open-minded and giving the girl a chance."

Annabelle snorts. "Yes, aren't you the altruistic one, giving girls in tight dresses the benefit of the doubt."

I knew she wasn't going to let the dress thing go. "Besides, why would I be open-minded about something stupid?" I ask.

"See?" she asks, pointing at me in triumph.

I shake my head in disgust. "That's not judgment; that's being logical in the face of stupidity."

"Yeah, it's not judgmental at all to call my interest stupid without even knowing anything about it."

"What's to know? A bunch of crap about how giant balls of white-hot gas can tell us the future? It's ridiculous, and you know it."

"If it's so ridiculous, then how come I keep winning my fantasy league?"

"Luck," I say firmly.

She shakes her head, her damp curls hanging in her face. "I don't know when you turned into such a stuck-up snob. I really don't..."

"And I don't know when you became such a total idiot!" But I know I've gone too far when I see her face. Her mouth snaps shut and her cheeks are pale. I'm about to apologize when she starts talking again, her voice a deadly calm.

"Astrology is a science. I'm sorry if you're too much of a thickheaded jock to see it," she says.

I'm very glad I didn't apologize. Once again, I'm having that very strange I've-been-beamed-into-an-alternate-universe feeling. Annabelle and I don't fight. We joke, we talk trash, we hold hands, we...But now she's talking to me like I'm a stranger. There's nothing I hate more than being called a dumb jock, and no one knows that better than Annabelle.

"But let's just stop talking about it," she continues. "Since we'll clearly never agree about it."

"Fine," I say stiffly. "Are we done here?"

"You're that eager to get back to your new girlfriend?" she asks.

Something about that word sets me off. It's...well, it's as if she's daring me to go after Sarah. But there's also something about her tone that mocks me, as though she thinks a girl like Sarah would never actually go out with a guy like me. And now I'm really seeing red.

"Maybe I am," I say, summoning all my self-control to sound calm. "Since I might as well find someone to enjoy the summer with."

I wish I'd kept my mouth shut; it hurts to say the words. It hurts even more to see Annabelle's face.

"So is that really it?" she asks, her lips trembling.

For a second, I pause. How can I possibly be through with Annabelle? She's been my fantasy *and* my best friend all in one since I was twelve years old. The moment I kissed her last summer was one of those rare, mystical events where real life exceeds dreams. It doesn't happen to most people, but it happened to me. I've thought about it every day since; I've waited all this time to be with her.

Then she speaks. "I thought we were meant to be. It's in the stars."

And just like that...the memory fades. Now I know what my answer is.

"I don't think it is in the stars. After all, I'm a Scorpio and you're a Leo, and everyone knows they don't mix." I'm just guessing since obviously I have no idea if they're a good match, but I can tell by Annabelle's face that my guess was spot on.

"That's just amateur astrology," she says irritably. "It doesn't take into account rising signs or birth charts or anything."

I almost laugh. Then I do. I can't help it. But it's a cold, miserable laugh, like the rain.

"Pete, are you coming back?"

Annabelle and I both turn and see Sarah coming toward us, a big, black umbrella protecting her from the pounding drizzle. Seeing it makes me realize I am soaked. And seeing her makes me realize that it is time to move on, past the new Annabelle and her endless talk about stars.

"Yes," I say. "I'm coming right now."

Jed Rogers

Born February 3: Aquarius ♒

Rising Sign: Cancer ♋

You are an eccentric who seeks out the unusual and unique. With the right match, you will remain true, despite your need for independence. But that drive for freedom can cause you to isolate yourself. This summer will see your business boom. Don't hide your true feelings behind that success, because come autumn you may have money but no special someone to spend it on.

chapter 6

He just left you standing there in the rain?"

Vanessa's voice is incredulous and makes my eyes well with tears. Again. Since my eyes are already swollen and sore from endless sleepless hours of crying, it's particularly painful. Though not as painful as telling Vanessa about what happened on the boardwalk last night—retelling it in real time is like reliving it.

Of course, she called first thing in the morning, worried because she had seen Pete and Sarah come back to the pool hall together. She tried me last night, but I wasn't able to talk then. And I'm starting to wonder if I'm really able to do it now. It's eight fifteen, but because I've barely slept, it feels more like three.

"What did I tell you?" she fumes, not waiting for an answer. "I can't believe he'd treat you like this. Actually, I can. Boys are jerks. End of story."

For once a bitter-shrew rant is actually making me feel slightly better about things. Pete *is* a jerk. I still can't believe he said the things he said, or how he would actually be remotely attracted to Sarah and her stupid tattoos. I mean, okay, maybe I said a couple of things I shouldn't have. I cringe every time I remember calling him a dumb jock—that was a hit below the belt. But the things he said to me were much worse. Much, *much* worse.

"Yeah," I mutter when Vanessa pauses.

"You know, in the end it's for the best," Vanessa says.

"How could Pete calling me a freak be for the best?" I ask, almost laughing in spite of my misery.

"Because he showed his true colors," she says. "Before this, there were hints at his jerkiness, but you were still tied to him. You needed solid proof. And last night you got it. He's not worth your time. It's that simple."

"I don't know. I just…can't believe it."

"Look at it this way," Vanessa says, and in the background I hear her turning pages of a newspaper. "This morning in the *New York Times* there was a story on the rise of teen pregnancy in Uganda. That could've been you if you'd kept on falling for Pete's act."

Now I do laugh. "Except that I don't live in Uganda. And I'm still a virgin, in case you forgot."

"That's irrelevant," she says impatiently. "The point is that all over the world girls are getting sweet-talked by jerky guys, and the guys sail off into the sunset while the girls are left with a shattered heart and possibly a child."

"Does the article say that all the guys are leaving the

girls?" I ask. "Maybe in Uganda guys are gentlemen and support their children and marry their girlfriends and don't leave them in the rain to go off with tattooed skanks."

Vanessa giggles but quickly clears her throat. "I didn't read the whole article, but you're totally missing what I'm saying. You're lucky to have found out about Pete now, before he ruined the summer and possibly the rest of your life."

"Maybe," I say. It doesn't feel lucky. It feels like a nightmare that I can't wake up from.

"I know it hurts right now," Vanessa says softly. "But believe me, you'll move on and have a great summer without him."

Why is it so completely impossible to imagine that? I can't picture anything in my life without Pete, especially not a summer in Gingerbread.

"It's a fresh start, a new and improved independent you," she says, sounding uncannily like Ms. Hearst, the mousy guidance counselor at my school.

"Is it bad that I hate being the new independent me?" I ask.

Luckily (or not), she doesn't hear me because she's off talking about how great it is for a girl to be standing on her own two feet with no guy to prop her up.

I guess I like props.

"We can be bitter shrews together," she concludes. "Maybe we can start an advice column in the *Gingerbread Post*."

"Not the *New York Times*?" I manage weakly, rolling over on my side and burrowing a little under my comforter.

"It'll be so popular it'll be picked up by papers all over," she says, using that mildly scary tone she uses when I can't tell if she's joking or not. "Though obviously not the *Times*. They only do serious stuff."

Becoming a bitter shrew seems serious to me. And honestly, I'm not even sure I'm feeling it. Depressed bunny or some other defenseless animal...that feels more like it. But maybe the bitter will come. "I should probably go," I say.

"Need to wallow in bed for a while?" she asks.

Man, she knows me well.

"That's allowed," she continues, "especially the first day. But tomorrow if you're still in bed in the same pajamas, I'm coming over and hauling you out and making you play volleyball with me at the Y."

There's nothing I hate more than playing organized sports with hardcore jocks like Vanessa's volleyball crowd, a fact she well knows. "Okay, okay—believe me, I'll get out of bed."

She laughs. "Good. I'll call you later to see how you're holding up. Oh, and Annabelle?"

"Yeah?"

"Lots of ice cream is allowed on day one. Chocolate too."

I almost manage a smile. "I'm so glad to hear it."

But when I click off the phone and fluff the comforter over me, the last thing in the world I want is to eat. Or to do anything really. Just lying here feels utterly exhausting. My insides feel like they've been hollowed out.

The thing I don't get is how the communication just... failed. Pete was the person I called when our dog Louie got hit by a car. When Gabe and I fought. When I blew my audition for *The Wiz* freshman year and was cast as "scenery" rather than the witch. (Which was actually funny in hindsight, but Pete was the one who made me see the humor in the situation.)

Pete listened to me cry and laugh; he said all the right things to make me feel better. Honestly, just knowing he was there, his voice soft and deep on the other end of the phone, made bad things bearable. Like saying good-bye to Gabe when he left for college. Or visiting Grandma Hillary in the hospital when she had a scare with her heart last year.

Pete is—*was*—my lifeline, my home base, and (yes, it's cheesy) my knight in shining armor. Knowing we could talk at anytime was like a shimmery coal I carried with me, burning bright on dark winter nights and keeping me warm and protected from the cold. I'm lost without that.

The tears have started again, sliding wet and salty down my cheeks. I don't bother to wipe them away because more will come. The supply seems endless at this point.

• • •

I wake up in the late afternoon and see something unusual out the window: sun. Wow. My eyes feel puffy and inflamed, and my stomach is sour from not eating since dinner last night. And the knowledge of Pete's disinterest weighs heavy on my chest, threatening to crush the air out of me all over again.

"Annabelle?" my mom calls, knocking on the door of my room. "Sweetie, are you okay? You've been in there all day."

I wish Mom had Gabe and Grandma Hillary or even some kind of summer preschool emergency to distract her from me. I clear my throat and try to make my voice sound as normal as possible. "Yeah, just getting some work done," I say. My mom is good about not coming into my room unless invited, so hopefully she'll think I've been reading astrology books all day or getting an early start on college applications.

"We're going to have a cookout for dinner since the weather is good, and I was thinking you and I could go pick up some clams and mussels from Uncle Joe's," she says. Uncle Joe's has the best fresh seafood in Gingerbread, maybe even on the planet. "But I don't want to interrupt if you're...busy. Or in a groove."

My cheek is resting against my pillow—still stained with wet spots from my tears. My pajamas are starting to sag from being worn too long, and my face is tight and raw. Really, there's no groove in sight.

"Yeah, I think I'll pass," I manage.

"Okay," she says. "Oh, and invite Pete to join us. If you want, I can call his parents and invite them all."

"No!" I bolt upright in bed. "I mean…his mom has a tight deadline, so I think the phone would disturb them. And Pete is, um, sick so he can't make it either."

"What a shame he's sick on such a beautiful day," my mom says. "But I guess that explains why you've been locked in your room all day."

Yes. It does. How convenient.

"I'll get some corn too," she adds, and I hear her start down the stairs.

"Great," I call, sinking back down into the pillows. I glance outside. It is beautiful, but honestly I wish it were raining. The bright sun feels mocking.

I roll over on one side and notice my laptop and the stack of worn astrology books on my nightstand. I am feeling hostile toward them since astrology is the cause of my fight with Pete…but is it really? No, I remind myself: the root cause is Pete being a stubborn snob.

I reach for my computer and log in to my favorite site, www.yourlifeiswritteninthestars.net, the one that has my birth chart on file so it's always extremely accurate about what's going on in my life at the moment. My laptop battery is low, but hopefully there's enough juice for me to get some insight into what is happening—and better yet, how I can fix it.

The screen dissolves into a horoscope: *This week is a week for business! It's time to ask for that promotion, put your nose to the grindstone with that big project, or start that small business you've been dreaming about.*

Okay, so not helpful. Though I shouldn't be surprised—yesterday's reading gave no notice that my world was about to explode. But seriously, business notes when my heart has been crushed to a pulp?

My phone vibrates with a text message. It's from Vanessa. I hear my dad stroll out to the front porch that overlooks the water to begin setting up the grill for the cookout. I turn over and close my eyes. I'm not up to dealing with any of it.

• • •

"I'm outside, I promise," I tell Vanessa, finally mustering the courage to answer when she calls the next morning. "No need for volleyball. I'm out in the world. I'm on the beach—listen, you can hear the waves." I hold up my cell phone toward the ocean to convince her. It's still sunny, truly a miracle for Gingerbread.

"Good," she says. "You have to be out for at least an hour."

"Why?" I whine. All I want is to crawl back under my comforter.

"For your mental health," she says firmly. "There was an article in the *Times* a few months ago about how exercise creates endorphins, which fight depression—"

"Vanessa, I'm sorry, but I really don't feel like hearing about the *Times* right now. Besides, it's going to take more than endolphins to keep me happy."

"Endorphins," she corrects, like I really care. "It's day three, Annabelle. There are no excuses on day three."

"Okay, a half hour," I promise. I close my phone and tuck it into the pocket of my sweat pants. I almost didn't bring these sweats since they are baggy and totally unflattering, but now I consider my last-minute decision to stuff them in my suitcase one of the best I've made in years. They are as close to pj's as clothing can get. The best part is that I can wear them right to bed when I get back.

I walk along the beach, my sneakers sinking slightly into the wet sand. So much for the sun…it's already clouding over. Within minutes, a few droplets turn to a steady drizzle. It feels cool on my cheeks. Maybe Vanessa is right. It does feel good to be out of bed. I trudge near the boardwalk and see the scarlet letters advertising Fred's Fabulous Funnel Cakes, and I realize I am in desperate need of deep-fried dough sprinkled with powdered sugar.

I'm taking my first bite when I see her. She's wearing a pair of jean capris so snug that they must make it hard for her blood to circulate and a blue halter top that shows off the tattoo on her shoulder. A huge black umbrella protects her from the rain that is running down my face and making my hair a puffball.

Suddenly the dough is like a ball of wet newspaper in my mouth, and all I want is to be hiding back in my room. Maybe she won't notice me and I can race home. I try to dash across the boardwalk to the steps that lead toward the beach, but it's too late.

"Well, hello," Sarah says as she steps carefully around a puddle. "Aren't you Pete's little friend?"

It's true: my five feet and two inches are no match for her heels and natural giraffe-like build.

"Yes, I'm Pete's *good* friend," I say, trying to make it sound mysterious. But the words fall flat on my own ears. Is that even true anymore?

The right side of her mouth curls up. "Right. Then maybe we'll see you at the party tonight. We're going to dinner first, though."

I can't believe this girl. *Really?* I feel like asking her. She's like a bad reality TV show come to life. And she's so smug she might as well just say, "He's mine now, so suck it." If Pete sees something in her…then yes, boys really *are* jerks.

"Pete is so thoughtful," she says. "Maybe it's being from a small town, but I've never been with a guy who brought me flowers on the first date."

Flowers? First date? The words echo in my ears, each bringing a new pang of anger and sadness. Sometime during my comatose solitude, Pete has managed to buy flowers and go on a date. With *her*. Why is she rubbing my face in this? He thinks she's hot; I get it, so let's move on. He has no feelings. He is a coldhearted—

"He's already checked the bus schedule from Vermont to New York so we can see each other in the fall."

Kill me now, please.

"That pastry you have looks good," she says, clearly not getting the hint to shut up or walk away, or both. "I wish I could afford to splurge on fattening things, but I'd be a whale if I did."

She runs a hand over her flat belly while eying my baggy sweats. They do have a rather whale-like quality. What is up with her? She got Pete; she wins the thinner-than-thou contest; but she's still staring at me, trying to find some other way to rip me down. Does she have some deep-seated need to ruin the lives of every female she sets eyes on? Because it's not like I did anything to her. Come to think of it, I've never even had a conversation with her before this.

"If you do ever want to lose a pound or two, I recommend the Martha's Vineyard cleanse. It's very holistic," she says. "Gets rid of toxins. Pete says you're into New Agey stuff, so I figured..." She doesn't finish.

And suddenly I get it. She *does* have something against me, something big. There's no way she'd treat me like this if I weren't a threat. And there's only one way I could threaten her: In addition to telling her that I'm into "New Agey stuff" (which I'm *not*; astrology doesn't count), Pete must have done or said something to tip her off that I was more than just a casual summer friend. She is marking her territory, hoping I will back off.

Inside, I have to admit, I am squealing with delight. But I remain calm. I take another bite of my dough and chew it slowly, then swallow. "Thanks, but I'm happy with how I look."

She arches an eyebrow, as if she couldn't possibly believe it.

"Have a great time at dinner," I say, turning and walking toward home.

For the first time since that horrible night, I feel hopeful that maybe, just maybe, Pete and I aren't through. If Sarah is acting this ridiculous, he must still feel something for me. And if that's the case, I'm not just going to roll over and give up. I'm going to fight. As I jog back home, my mind brimming with schemes and plans, I remember my astrology prediction...the one about business.

It's spot on.

• • •

It takes me two days to develop my plan—two days of begging my parents for money (I promise to pay back the $400 with interest), getting mixed up in the Gingerbread Beach summer real estate rental market (my parents have to sign the lease), and another day to corner Pete at the Opera Café. (My parents, convinced I've lost my mind, are very relieved to have me out of the house.) My heart aches when I see Pete, his curls damp from the rain, as he chats with Jed at the counter.

"Hey," I say.

His eyes light up for the briefest moment when he sees me. Then they go distant and blank, but I know what I saw.

"I have a proposition for you," I continue, emboldened.

Jed shoots Pete an indecipherable stare and then walks over to the back fridge for supplies to give us a moment alone.

Pete nods, not quite looking at me. "What is it?"

"Well, you're convinced that astrology is junk, and I'm convinced it's the real deal. So let's see who's right."

He almost smiles. "How are we going to do that?" he asks. I can hear just a flicker of interest in his voice.

"I rented out a storefront," I tell him. "Right on the boardwalk. You and I are going to start an astrology booth. We'll read people's charts for romance and see what happens. If we make a bunch of happy couples and the place gets mobbed, we know I'm right. And if it's a complete bust, you win and I'll never say another word about astrology."

Pete's brows slowly rise and then twist into a knot. "You want…us start an astrology advice booth together? I don't think so."

At that very moment, Sarah hurries through the door of the café and lowers her umbrella, looking around for Pete.

I don't have much time. Pete is already going back to his coffee, totally unconvinced. So I pull out my surefire ace in the hole and look Pete straight in the eye.

"You and me and an astrology booth. I dare you."

Daisy Lin

Born June 6: Gemini ♊

Rising Sign: Leo ♌

Your wit and warmth attract people to you, making your life rich with friendship and love. The lightning-fast way you change your mind can surprise others, but once you open your heart to the right person, you are trustworthy and genuine. This summer's motto must be "Seize the day." Tensions that seem hostile can hide romantic possibility: don't be blind to that because then opportunity will slip through your fingers.

chapter 7

Even as I'm walking to the boardwalk for the first day at our astrology booth, the whole thing still feels like a huge practical joke. I actually poked my head into Daisy's Realty the day after Annabelle dared me to go into "business" to ask if Annabelle had indeed rented the same broken-down shack where Larry used to run his laser-tag scam. Not only had she rented it; Daisy informed me that had already named it: "The Star Shack."

That's it, I thought. *She's lost it completely.*

On the other hand, she was still sane enough to dare me (which she knew I would never be able to turn down)... so here I am, up before nine on a stormy morning, making my way to the shack of stars. Good times ahead, I'm sure. Though really we'll weave a few fortunes; people will get pissed that we don't know what we're talking about; and in a week, I'll be back to my life.

As I walk down the boardwalk, I can't help smiling: for a second, I remember that first moment of seeing Annabelle brandishing a laser-tag gun and waving it at Larry. But the warm glaze of memory lifts fast when I see the words on the wooden sign she has hung up. It spells out "Star Shack" in big letters with all these little symbols painted around it that must be astrology mumbo jumbo. Annabelle is not the most gifted artist, so it's a little sloppy—but you get the gist.

And as I get closer, I see a sign on the door that says, "Get your love horoscope for ten dollars, and find your perfect match written in the stars."

Puke.

I push open the door. I half expect to see Annabelle wearing a turban or a long gauzy skirt, but she just looks her usual gorgeous self in a pink T-shirt and faded cutoffs. Not that I notice the gorgeous part. Or how her hair is pulled back in some kind of fancy braid so her blue eyes look even bigger.

"What do you think?" Annabelle asks, smiling, and for a second I fall into it and smile back.

But then I get a hold of myself and glance around the booth. She's hung tapestries on the walls and put up posters of constellations. There is also a big picture of Cupid shooting an arrow that I know she got as a joke, but I'm not going to get suckered into laughing about it because, really, this whole place is a joke.

"It's fine," I say in a monotone.

She looks disappointed, but she had to know the last thing I'd do is get all excited about the décor. Even if it were a baseball booth, getting psyched about décor is not my thing.

"Well, anyway, this is where we'll sit," she says, gesturing to a table she's set up in the middle of the tiny room. There are two folding chairs behind it and one in front, for a customer I guess, if we even get any.

"I made up a form for people to fill out with their birth information." She points to a clipboard neatly filled with half-page forms next to a pink mug filled with pens. "We can't do a whole birth chart since that would take forever, but I have what we need for reading the seventh house and rising signs and stuff."

I shrug since she may as well be speaking Russian. I start thinking about Sarah. We kissed for the first time at Jed's party, and while it wasn't some major religious experience, it was still awesome.

The one drawback was that Sarah kept harping on how I shouldn't fall into Annabelle's "trap" of accepting the dare. But whatever. Like I said: we'll be over and done with it as soon as people see what a huge crock it is. Then Sarah and I will move on to *real* conversation. I've only known her a little over a week, I remind myself. Things are moving plenty fast.

"And I brought a few books for reference," Annabelle adds, laying them out on the table.

"Wait…you need books? I thought you were an expert."

Her cheeks flush. She glares at me. "It's not something you just pick up from the back of a cereal box. It takes years to learn, and even hardcore astrologers use reference books. Doctors use reference books too, you know."

I grin a little at her defensiveness. "Right. Doctors."

"So do chemists and physicists," she says. "Even baseball coaches."

"Sure, they do," I grumble, but unfortunately I know she's right. Not that I mention what I know about baseball managers' reading habits.

The rain is pelting down hard, and it thuds on the tin roof of the booth. It's a soothing sound, though I notice a small leak toward the back of the booth that has water pooling in a corner. Oh, well. If there's a flood, we get to close early.

"So what do we do now?" I ask.

"Wait for customers, I guess," she says. "I'm sure we'll get some soon. I hung fliers around and left a pile of them in the Opera Café and Freddy's Fabulous."

But after twenty minutes, it's still just us, stilted silence, and the rain.

"Maybe I'll go and actually *hand out* some fliers," Annabelle says. "Just to get things started."

She heads out into the stormy day with her whale umbrella, and I slouch down in one of the folding chairs. The chair is hard metal, and a loose screw is poking into my back. I shift, and my elbow brushes against one of her books. This one has a pie chart on the front split into twelve slices with the signs of the zodiac. I flip it open and notice that it's worn and dog-eared. For a second, I flash on Annabelle reading it late at night, in bed, in her pj's, her hands turning the pages, maybe brushing a curl out of her face as she reads.

She takes this stuff seriously. Amazing.

With a jolt, I realize that I am on the verge of looking like a complete moron. It's a dare, but I have to play fair. We are doing this booth together. I need to at least know *a little* about astrology.

I turn to the table of contents and see there is a breakdown of each of the twelve zodiac signs. Good thing I'm a fast reader. But as I start flipping through the pages, I begin to feel lost. I know I'm a Scorpio, so I look up what it says about that. There's a man-woman breakdown, so I flash to "Scorpio Man."

> The Scorpio Man burns with passion. But on the outside, he is calm, cool, and collected. If you're thinking about double-crossing him, don't. He'll explode. When he loves, he loves forever. So if you're the object of his fire, it will never die or fall to cinders. He is smart, emotional (though he hides it), philosophical, and a lover of life. He goes overboard when it comes to eating, drinking, and romance. If he wants to live in luxury, he will.

Wow. That's actually...okay, no, that's *not* accurate. Who *wouldn't* want to live in luxury? And yes, I'm passionate about the Red Sox and baseball and—

I quickly look up Leo: Annabelle's sign.

> Leo: You are full of courage and creativity, generous with love, and know your strengths. Those include (perhaps too much) self-confidence. You don't like complications. You admire individuality and strive for it in yourself. You don't respond well to people who don't share your complete enthusiasm and creative spirit. Your oversensitivity to personal criticism makes you fly into a rage. You are, in a word, stubborn. You hold onto a belief or stick to a course of action through thick and thin. You are proud, outgoing, happy, kind, generous, self-expressive, intelligent, and broad minded.

The door opens. Annabelle is back. I stuff the book under the table so she won't know I've been reading it.

"No one interested in our little business venture?" I choke out. "I can't say I'm surprised."

She shoots me a sour look. "The rain is letting up a bit so I'm sure we'll be mobbed in no time."

"Sweet!" I laugh uncomfortably, not sure if I'm mocking her or if I suddenly buy into this crap.

"I'm gonna get some coffee," she says. "Want a cup?"

"Uh..."

"I know what you want," she says in a strange tone, and she's off again, fliers in hand.

I go back to my reading and hope that there is a line at Opera. If I can just get through the basics about each sign and then look up rising signs and the seventh house or whatever…I'll be okay. Or did she say sixth house? How many houses are there? I should have Googled all this before I showed up today…

It's almost half an hour before she is back, and I've gotten through a lot of it, including a segment on what signs match up well. Scorpios and Leos are a no-no in terms of a match—in both the Leo *and* Scorpio sections, *and* for both women and men. I can't help but feel oddly pissed off.

Plus, there's a section that gives advice for each sign. It's actually sort of funny. Not intentionally, but the tips tend to read far less accurately than the sign traits. (One Scorpio horoscope: "Don't fear love. It will come.") Now I'm eager for my coffee. I'm enjoying my first sip when Annabelle sits down and clears her throat.

"So how's Sarah?" she asks. "Did she get you that beer yet?"

"Yeah, she did." A lie: I hate beer, and Annabelle knows it. At the party, I kept spilling, pretending I was already drunk. "We had a great time this weekend."

Annabelle snorts. "I'm sure it was a wild time."

"It was great," I say. "Sarah is really smart, and she loves baseball."

"Does she now?" Annabelle asks skeptically.

Actually she has a right to be skeptical since Sarah isn't a real fan. It's more like she thinks the Red Sox jersey is cute. But hey, *she* looks cute in it, and it's better than a girl who likes wearing a Yankees shirt.

"I know you buy into all the stereotypes about tattoos," I say. "But you're wrong about Sarah. She's very down to earth, and we have a great time together."

Correction, not for Annabelle: I know we *will* have a great time once Sarah and I hang out a little more. She can't always talk the whole night about how she met the lead singer of (now I can't even remember), right? And it's just a fluke that she hates punk. She probably just hasn't been exposed to the good stuff.

"Well, I'm glad," Annabelle says.

"Me too. It's a relief to have normal conversation with someone," I say, staring pointedly at the pile of astrology books.

"You know, sometimes you..." Annabelle begins, turning in her chair to glare at me head on.

"What? Sometimes I *what*? Annabelle, you have to—"

"Um, excuse me," a timid voice says.

Annabelle and I both turn toward the front of the booth. It's Daisy Lin—the very same Daisy who gave Annabelle the lease. She's always friendly...though, as I think about it, I mostly see her by herself. She's in her early thirties, with long black hair and a T-shirt emblazoned with *I Sing for Love.*

Yikes. Maybe that's why she's always alone?

"Are you guys open?" she asks.

"Yes, absolutely," Annabelle says, beaming and reaching out her hand to welcome our very first customer. "Are you here about the property—"

"No. I'm here for..." She doesn't finish.

"Great! Just fill out this birth-date information, and we'll give you a reading."

"Thanks." She avoids Annabelle's eyes, talking as if she's on a job interview. "Not that I'm one of those people desperate to find a boyfriend or anything..."

"Of course not," Annabelle says.

Daisy smiles. "But I'd love to find someone as perfect for me as you guys are for each other."

Now I want to crawl under the folding chair and die. I've never seen Daisy smile before. There is a very long, very awkward pause.

"So, yeah, here's the form," Annabelle finally says.

Daisy scribbles onto the form, and I read it upside down as she writes. Born June 6—that means she's a Gemini. I quickly think through the things I read about Geminis and their matches. Daisy hands Annabelle the form with a ten-dollar bill and looks at her expectantly.

Annabelle turns to me with a smirk. "Pete, want to kick things off for Daisy?"

I can tell she's planned this as a typical Annabelle-one-ups-Pete moment, and it makes me smile, because—what do you know?—I have some knowledge, and even when we are barely speaking, I can't deny the kick in surprising her.

"Sure," I say, casually. "Let's see…you're a Gemini. That means you're a thinker. You love ideas and making them happen. You change your mind fast, but you're loyal when you find true love."

Daisy is nodding like I've said something incredibly insightful, which is kind of cool, actually. It makes me feel as if I wasn't a complete idiot about what I'd just read about my own signs—or that I'm an idiot spouting garbage about stars that seem to indicate you're a total genius. (How else could you interpret "thinker?")

The shock on Annabelle's face is too priceless. She's gaping at me as if I'm a stranger.

"You're independent though, Daisy," I continue, adding her name for personal emphasis. "So you can't be with a sign that needs constant attention. I'm thinking maybe Libra or Aquarius. You see, they're air signs, like you. And air signs share…what's the term I'm looking for? Let's say intellectual curiosity."

I'm pretty much reciting the book word for word, but Daisy is staring at me as if I'm an old-time Biblical prophet. I have to admit: I'm kind of liking this. I close my eyes for a second, trying to remember the advice for Gemini. The chart in the back had a breakdown of the whole year…there was something specific about summer…

"The thing that's keeping you from finding your match this summer is tension with the right person," I conclude, opening my eyes and fixing her with a meaningful stare. "You need to look past your surface conflict and see the true connection."

Daisy jumps up. "You're incredible!" she says, reaching over the table to hug me. "This is just what I needed," she adds, more calmly but still beaming. "I think I knew before coming in…but hearing you tell me is a shot in the arm. And that stuff about me being independent! That's what I've been doing wrong, getting with guys who were too clingy."

"Knowing the kinds of personality traits that suit you can make such a difference in finding a match," Annabelle chimes in.

"Yes," Daisy says, nodding. "There has to be a basic compatibility there." She leans over and pecks me on the cheek. "And thanks to you, I know exactly where to go to find it!"

"We're so glad we could help," Annabelle says, glaring at me. "Remember to tell your friends about us."

Daisy is already out the door. "Oh, I will, believe me!" she calls.

I lean back in the chair and fold my arms across my chest, grinning.

"How did you do that?" Annabelle asks, in what sounds like real awe.

I shrug. "What can I say? I'm just good."

Annabelle's eyes narrow, and she gives me a hard look and then glances around the storefront. "No computer, so you didn't get it there," she says to herself. Then she looks at the books. "Of course. Your freakish, verging-on-photographic memory. You were reading about astrology while I was out."

"Please," I scoff weakly.

"It was just beginner's luck," she says. "Daisy already knew what she needed to do, but with the hard cases, you'll just have to watch the expert in action."

I snort.

She lifts an eyebrow. "Believe me, when things get tough, your little cram session will be useless."

"I guess we'll see," I say, my hackles rising. I reach out and grab another book, not caring if she sees. And all at once, I'm committed. No date with Sarah tonight. Nope, forget it. I'll cancel. I'm going home to learn everything online I can about astrology. There's no way Annabelle is going to one-up me in this. Seriously, if I can get a hug from Daisy with less than an hour of reading, who knows what else I can do?

John Peterson

Born March 12: Pisces ♓

Rising Sign: Libra ♎

Your intuition serves you when you stay grounded, but your tendency to dream can leave you detached and alone. The right person will appreciate your kindness and sensitivity and celebrate your insights to others and yourself. This summer, you need to lose the ego. Pride will be your downfall, so don't be afraid to take the risk of saying what you truly feel.

chapter 8

I've been scowling at Pete for a while now. He is thumbing furiously through *Astrology Matches for Love Everlasting.* I mean, yeah, he recited stuff from the book (I knew it sounded familiar), but there's a lot in there and he knew exactly what to tell Daisy.

Those books all have an overflow of info in them…and for him to parse through it…and find exactly the right things to give Daisy her match advice—that's not just memorization, that's skill. Whether he likes it or not, Pete has a head for astrology. But I'm sure he doesn't even realize it. He's scamming me to win the dare.

"Hey!" A tall, college dude ducks in the door out of the rain. I've seen him around, and I think his name is John. He's got messy black hair and horn-rimmed glasses and a too-tight, button-down short-sleeved shirt. He reeks of *The Daily Show* and worthwhile leftist causes and obscure emo. (Maybe that's mean, but astrologists deal in absolutes.) He has a newspaper tucked under his arm.

"So you guys can help me find my perfect match, huh?"

"That's the goal," I say, smiling and ignoring that fact that his question was half-sarcastic. Why do guys have such issues with astrology? Or just admitting that they need help in the love department, period?

John sits down. "I'm the hardest case you'll have this summer." He takes a ten out of his wallet and hands it to me.

"Why?" I ask, and I am being earnest.

"Because I don't believe in love," he says.

He seems serious. I might as well buy into it.

"I'm not sure it exists at all," he goes on. "I think it's a social construct invented by our forefathers to get the human race to breed."

Pete is nodding, but I roll my eyes. "Please," I say. "If you really believed that, you wouldn't be here."

John laughs a little. "Okay, you've got me there. Maybe I do think love could exist. But I'm not sure it can exist for me."

"Why is that?" I ask him.

He smiles wryly. "The usual. I got my heart handed to me on a platter by my ex-girlfriend."

"Well, I think we can help you make that a distant memory," I say confidently. "Go ahead and fill out your birth-date information, and we'll see what we can do."

Next to me, Pete is looking at John's sheet, nodding as John fills out his birthday and the town where he was born: the Bronx. *Home of the Yankees!* I realize, and my mind suddenly clouds. I see that he was born on March 2, and for a second I blank out, trying to remember what sign that makes him…I can't believe it. My mind is suddenly a sieve.

Before I can get a handle on it, John is passing us the form and Pete is looking at me, a challenging expression on his face. "Annabelle, want to take this one?"

And just like that, I'm flustered. Normally I'd just open up one of my books and start there. "Um, March second," I say, "that would be…Aquarius?"

As soon as it's out of my mouth, I know it's wrong. Pete says the word before I can: "Pisces, Annabelle. Actually, it's Pisces." He flashes me a brittle smile and turns to John. "Sorry, it's our first day…you were saying?"“

Great. Just great.

"I'm sorry," John says, his puzzled gaze flashing between the two of us. "Which one of you is giving me advice?"

"I am," I pipe up. "So, yes, Pisces…" The thing is, I'm rattled now and it's hard to think. "You tend to dream big, which is great," I begin.

"Well, John, except for how those big dreams might rub some people the wrong way, which I'm thinking might have led to your past girlfriend problems," Pete interjects.

I shoot him a look, but John is nodding. "Yeah," he says. "It really bugged Brenda that I'd talk about wanting to do the Peace Corps. But now I don't want to do that anymore. Can I be serious?"

"Of course," Pete says, in a somber tone, so over the top that I want to gag.

"I want to become a reporter to expose injustice in the world."

Pete nods as if this makes perfect sense. "See, you need a girl like you: someone who's looking past the moment, who wants to make a difference."

"Exactly!" John says excitedly. "So how do I find her?"

Pete looks at me with an expression of pure bliss—which I actually find sort of cute—and now I'm a total mess. I shake my head.

"Well, since you're a…ah…I mean, based on your birthday and year, I think you're ruled by Saturn, which—"

"Actually, Annabelle, I'm not sure Pisces on that date *is* ruled by Saturn. I think I remember it being something else."

Pete grabs *Astrology in Love and War,* flips to a page in the middle, and squints, nodding thoughtfully. At this point, I honestly can't even tell if he's joking or smug or what.

"Yes, I was right…You're ruled by Venus, which means you have the energy and drive to make a relationship happen this summer—a relationship with someone who wants to make a change in the way that you do. A change not only for yourselves, but for the world."

"Great," John says, so eagerly I'd smile if I weren't a defeated heap sitting next to the astrological wonder that used to be Pete.

"Your matches are going to be other water signs," I say, hoping to get back in the game. "Think Cancer and Scorpio."

"You know, I wonder…" Pete scratches his chin.

Okay, he can't challenge me on this. Pisces is water, and water signs are the best match: period.

"It's true that generally water goes with water, but in your case, I'm thinking it might be different," Pete goes on. "I mean, you have the whole save-the-world thing happening, which makes me think you're one of those water people who will actually do better with air signs."

I can feel my mouth drop open because he's spot on. John has a rising Libra, which gives him certain qualities that *will* match up better with an air sign.

"I'm thinking Aquarius," Pete concludes. "Do you agree, Annabelle?"

"Uh…"

"She agrees," Pete says.

"Wow, thanks, you guys," John says, standing up. "I'm starting to believe maybe there is hope for me in the love department. You know, I have to admit…"

"Let me guess," Pete interrupts, shaking his hand. "You weren't sure whether or not to trust in astrology. Believe me, we've all been there."

Now I realize I want to kill Pete Riley.

"Just one last piece of advice," Pete says. "Watch the ego.

You don't want to let your pride get in the way of what your heart wants."

"Got it," John concurs, nodding thoughtfully.

Again Pete is quoting the stupid book and making himself into an astrological superhero. While I, the supposed expert, sit useless and speechless by his side. How did this happen, again? Oh, right: me and my stupid dare. But wait…isn't Pete just sabotaging himself by going along with me? Doesn't he *want* this to fail?

"Not bad for a first day," Pete says, grinning as John steps out.

Before I can answer or ask any more questions, we hear the clomping sound of footsteps muffled by rain. We both look toward the door, expecting to see a tour group headed for the Opera Café. But this stampede isn't for food. It's a group of four college students (first-timers to Gingerbread), followed by five high school girls (regulars whom I barely know), followed by others I can hear but can't yet see. They are all stopping right here at the Star Shack.

This stampede is for us.

• • •

"In the end, it just means that you want to avoid the Capricorn guy, the alpha who needs to be in charge," Pete concludes, smiling at the blond cheerleader type who is sitting across the table from him and lapping up his every word. She doesn't even glance my way. But why should she?

It's day three of the Star Shack, and the crazy crowds—first started by Daisy and quickly followed by dozens of others that we (well, *Pete*) have helped—have not abated. There's been a line outside the door the past two mornings, even today when the rain was much more than the typical Gingerbread drizzle. Under other circumstances, I'd be thrilled by our success. But since it's coinciding with my own personal failure, I'm…ambivalent.

The blond girl leaves, practically slobbering on Pete as she goes, and our next customer comes in: a girl our age named Carmen who sometimes takes shifts at the Opera Café. She's always struck me as nice, friendly, and giggly but not the sharpest claw in the clam bucket.

"Hi," she says as she sits down in the customer chair opposite our table. "I hear you guys are going to be the answer to all my guy problems."

Pete smiles this new smile he has: a kind of knowing and mysterious grin that tells people he has incredible insight. It's annoying on its own, but coupled with the fact that he actually *does* have insight, it's beyond exasperating.

"It's so cute you guys are in love so you started this booth to help other people find romance," Carmen says, which quickly wipes the smile off Pete's face and has me fumbling for the form.

That's the other thing: everybody in this tiny town thinks we've started this business to share our own brand of special love—which doesn't exist. The only exception to this rule is Tattoo Sarah, of course, who lurks outside the door whenever we're about to close, glaring at me and muttering to herself, waiting to whisk Pete away the second he steps outside.

"Here," I say. "Just give us your birth info, and we'll give you your reading."

Carmen jots down the date, time, and place, and then hands me the form and her crumpled ten-dollar bill.

"Okay, October 12...that makes you a Libra." I raise my voice, trying to drown out the noise of the muttering line outside and to distract myself from the intensity of Carmen's gaze—and most of all, to distract myself from Pete, who sits waiting, coiled and ready for me to make a mistake so he can take over.

I am at a total loss as to how or why it's possible that I—who have used astrology for years—cannot give a single piece of advice past what you'd find in the daily paper's horoscope, while Pete, who still calls astrology "freakish," is coming up with the most perceptive advice available outside of Oprah.

Carmen nods. "Right. I'm all about balance."

"Which is a great thing and can serve you well in relationships," I concur. I want to put all thought into October 12 and what that means in terms of Venus, but it's hard with Pete bearing down on me, leaning just close enough that I can smell his peppermint shampoo and the Tide his mom uses on their laundry. Suddenly I'm overcome with nostalgia. How can a girl focus on anything? Not to mention the fact that he's just waiting for me to screw up…

I look at Carmen's birth year and then flip open a book. "Your Venus is in Virgo, which makes you a perfectionist in love."

"Totally," she says, nodding.

Okay, this is good. I'm on the right track. "And you can be reserved, waiting for guys to take initiative rather than going for it yourself," I say, still cribbing from the book. But as soon as the words are out of my mouth, I know I'm wrong.

This is the thing about astrology: You have different elements—sun signs and rising signs and houses and planets—and every one offers insight, but you have to take it all in a big-picture way…seeing how maybe some tendencies are less developed while others are dominant. That's where the insight (which Pete is so good at and I apparently suck at) comes in. Because anyone with observation skills can tell that Carmen is not reserved at all; she's got the social part of Libra kicked into high gear.

I don't want to look up, but I know I have to. When I do, I see Carmen's doubtful expression and Pete grinning.

"Actually, I think Carmen is a flirt in the best way possible," he says, and she turns away from me to look at him. "I think you are all about charm."

Carmen shakes her head, but anyone with eyes can see she's pleased. And that Pete's right.

I sigh and sink down in my metal chair. I look at the line of eager people standing at the door and trailing out and then close my eyes, wishing the day was over and I was in bed reading a book about anything—*anything*—except astrology.

• • •

My astrology slump is ten days and counting, while Pete's winning streak is still going strong. But still, today, for some reason, I feel confident. Maybe it's the rare sun. The change in the dismal weather means something good, that things are going to take a turn in my direction for once. They have to.

I mutter a "Hey" to the people already congregating outside the Star Shack and then head inside to where Pete is waiting.

"Ready?" he asks.

I sit down in the metal chair and try to pretend like it's the first time I'm doing so. It's a fresh start. This is *my* shack, in *my* name, after all (well, technically my parents')—but still, Pete is just along for the ride. I take a deep breath and nod.

Pete opens the door and beckons in the first customer: a guy we've never seen before (weekend visitor, up to see some tourist?) with shaggy hair decked out in a faded T-shirt and frayed cargo shorts.

"So I want to find me some *lo-o-ve*," he coos, leering at me as he sits down.

I pass him the form while Pete says, "I hear you, brother," and they high five. Pete has this irritating way of putting on different personas with different customers. Like with certain girls, he's all "sensitive." But with caveman types, he's slapping palms and laughing at burps and chuckling at stupid sexual innuendos that they seem to think I'm too thick to get.

I roll my eyes and wait for *Mr. Lo-o-ve* to finish scrawling sloppily on his form and to hand it over to me.

"Okay...Wilson." I squint, barely able to read his handwriting. "You're a Leo, which is a fire sign."

"I could have told you that," he says, winking.

"Yeah, so anyway, that means you do well with other fire signs."

"True dat." He laughs. "I like my women hot."

"Actually the fire part is about spirit. Like being energetic and idealistic."

Wilson frowns. "I don't really like chicks who get all preachy or want to climb mountains," he says. "I'm just looking for fun."

What a shocker. I'm about to speak my mind when Pete holds up a hand.

"I think you want more than that," Pete says. "I'm thinking you're a Leo who can handle a Scorpio." He makes it sound like Wilson has what it takes to date a rock star.

"Not a lot of guys can handle a Scorpio woman because they're intense, but they match that with true passion."

Wilson is nodding, his eyes bright. "Yeah, I'd be all over that," he says.

As Pete drones on about passion, and the bright sunlight filters through the mobbed doorway, I realize I was very wrong: nothing is going to change. At least I managed to avoid the metal chair with the loose screw today. I think that is about all that's going to go my way, though.

• • •

At the end of the day as we're just about to leave, Pete suddenly draws in a sharp breath. I turn—and then I gasp too. Standing in the doorway is Jed, the man known for never leaving his shop, who won't even own a dog because he says that relationship would take too much time away from his café.

But he isn't alone.

Jed is holding hands with a woman.

Holding hands…and smiling and gazing at her like she's more wonderful than a fresh cappuccino with the finest coffee beans ever harvested in the history of coffee harvesting. But even that is not the truly shocking part. The part that has both Pete and me staring speechless is the woman. Because we know her. More than that, we know her birth chart.

Jed is holding hands with Daisy Lin, Gingerbread Beach's realtor.

Aisha Wright

Born May 1: Taurus ♉

Rising Sign: Gemini ♊

You are down to earth and set in your ways, and your dependability makes you a valued friend. You are slow to open your heart, but once you do, you love with everything you've got. This summer, watch out for your tendency to make things harder on yourself than they need to be.

chapter 9

"Seriously, I was so wasted I could barely walk," Sarah says, laughing like she's said something funny and kicking her legs (just a little too violently) to make our Ferris wheel car swing. "I don't even remember how I got home."

For the ninetieth time, I am hearing the story of how Sarah got drunk at her senior prom. Is it a good story? No. Is there any reason she should be telling it to me every single time we hang out? No. But can I do anything to stop it? Apparently not. I actually fell so low as to try and talk about the weather (the weather!) to avoid it. But like the rain of Gingerbread, the prom story is frequent and unavoidable. At least it's better than the tattoo conversation...

"What a wild night," she muses, suddenly snuggling against me, which has the odd effect of making the car of the Ferris wheel swing even more. I realize right then that we are high up. The boardwalk stretches far below, damp with earlier rain, the sun setting over the hills to the west, the gray ocean spreading out to the east...There's a creak, and I flinch. I think this Ferris wheel was made before even Annabelle's Grandma Hillary was born.

"Hah, you scared?" she asks.

"Um..." I ease my arm around her, even though I'm not really feeling like it. I turn my head so my face isn't close to her hair—she uses this patchouli shampoo that makes my eyes water. But snuggling is preferable to talking.

"It's so nice up here," she breathes.

"You mean...in the Ferris wheel?"

"No, silly!" But she doesn't bother to elaborate. She rubs my palm in a way that should turn me on (I think?) but instead feels mildly irritating, like having an ant on my hand. I've been waiting for chills—*real* chills, Annabelle-caliber chills, falling-in-love chills—with Sarah. But I figure that kind of thing takes time. Then again, the only experience I've ever had is with Annabelle...and she never bugged me in the way Sarah does. At least, not at first.

"So what did you do today?" she asks, now bored.

The Ferris wheel is rotating back to the ground, and after a few more long seconds, we're able to make our escape. The wet boardwalk feels very solid under my feet.

"Um...after the Star Shack, I watched the game," I finally answer. I keep hoping if I talk about baseball enough, she'll start to get into it.

She scowls. "You need to give that astrology thing a rest. You won the dare, Pete. You should quit while you're ahead."

"It's no big deal. But speaking of winning, the Sox won in the ninth, so that was great."

Sarah looks down and inspects her nails. "I bought hair dye today. How do you think I'll look as a redhead?"

"Great," I say. One thing I've learned at the Star Shack: certain questions don't require thought; they just need to be answered right. Though you'd think if I can fake interest in her hair color, she could fake interest in the Red Sox…

"What do you want to do next?" I ask her as she reaches for my hand.

"How about you win me a teddy bear?" she says.

It's all I can do to suppress a groan. Annabelle has a thing about girls who want guys to win them prizes (and so do I, come to think of it), so we had a tradition where every year she'd win *me* something. Annabelle has a wicked pitching arm from her Little League days, so she'd get to the highest level. I'd be stuck carrying a huge giraffe or pink rabbit around the rest of the night. I have a stash of them in my bedroom at home.

"You're so strong," Sarah says, squeezing my arm. "I know you can do it." She tilts her face up for a kiss.

Why do I want to run away? Aside from the fact that every word out of her mouth is like bad dialogue from some terrible teen movie? But why am I thinking about Annabelle? I'm here with this sexy college girl who's crazy about me. True, the chemistry isn't smoking. But maybe in time it will be.

I lean down and kiss her back. And as I do, I'm aware of people walking by and the taste of fennel toothpaste—I don't get why anyone would clean their mouth out with the flavor of licorice—and I realize that I'm only thinking of all the stuff that's supposed to melt into the background. With Sarah, the *kissing* is the background. And that can't be good.

She pulls back, smiles at me, and then starts walking toward the row of game booths. I follow reluctantly.

"Yo, Pete!" a familiar voice calls down the boardwalk.

I turn to see Bill and Dave, part of the High-Five-"Dude!" set that Scott and Ben and most of the other summer regulars belong to. They're familiar faces at every keg party Saturday night and every hungover Sunday at the Opera Café.

"What's up?" I say, stopping to chat. Maybe if we talk long enough, Sarah will forget about the games.

"Just hanging," Bill says.

"So I hear you and Annabelle started the busiest booth of the summer," Dave says. "Pretty smart selling love advice when you guys are the couple of the century."

Why does everyone still think we're together? I may work in an astrology booth, but I don't date astrology freaks. And I go everywhere with Sarah—who is standing right here, obviously with me. How is it possible to miss this? Before I can set them straight, a group of girls walk by and the guys are instantly distracted.

"Well...catch you later," Bill says.

I pull Sarah close and kiss her, hoping they will see and realize once and for all that Annabelle and I are history. But when I look up, the guys have turned the corner and just strangers are walking past.

"So are you going to win me my tiger?" Sarah asks. She growls a little. Actually growls. I can feel my face turning red.

"I guess," I mutter.

As we walk toward the games, the misty rain kicks in again, switching quickly to actual drops.

"Oh, we better go," Sarah says.

"It's okay. Most stuff stays open in the rain," I say.

"No!" she barks, her eyes flashing with anger. "Look at these boots, idiot! You think I want to get them wet?"

I blink several times, at a loss. "Uh..."

She shakes her head and starts toward the parking lot where I left my car. Last summer, Annabelle and I were going on rides when it started to pour. It was practically a hurricane, and pretty much everyone else was leaving. But we got tickets to the bouncy ball place for kids and spent the afternoon pelting each other with big plastic balls and sliding around on the bouncy floor as we got totally soaked. But whatever. That was last year, and if Sarah wants to get her precious boots out of the rain, it's fine. In fact, it's good because I don't have to win her the stupid tiger.

And I really need to stop thinking about Annabelle.

Sarah is already in the car when I catch up. I slam the door behind me and sit behind the wheel for a moment, wiping the rain from my face. I'm expecting her to be angry, but she's smiling as if nothing happened.

"What's this I see?" she asks, holding something up in one hand.

It takes me a minute to identify it. "Oh, a ski-lift ticket," I say. I'm about to explain that it's my mom's and that she left it in my car when Sarah reaches over and squeezes my arm.

"Of course you're a skier—I should have known! I love to ski," she says. "We'll have to go in the fall."

This is why I keep thinking about Annabelle. Because she was totally right about Sarah. And I hate her for it.

• • •

"So I just can't thank you guys enough," the woman with blond hair says, grinning at Annabelle. "He's perfect, a Sagittarius, just like you recommended," she adds, nodding at me. "We're totally in love. Seriously, we're almost as perfect for each other as you guys are."

She leaves before either of us can correct her—which is both completely annoying and all too common. It's been almost a week since my carnival trip with Sarah, but this, right here, is the reason I decided not to break up with her after realizing we have zero chemistry and zero in common. People are going to think Annabelle and I are a couple forever unless I can show the world I've moved on. And I need to show Annabelle too.

Plus, if I'm honest, I have to admit breaking up with Sarah would be a nightmare I'm not sure I could handle right now. She's already given me train and bus schedules so we can visit each other in the fall, and she texts me literally every hour. *What r u doing? xoxo* (Answer: Hoping you won't text.) And after the off-kilter boots incident, I'm not sure I want to see extended anger…the kind of anger that happens when a person gets dumped.

"Hey," an unfamiliar skater-dude says, poking his head in the door. He's skinny with long, dark bangs. "Can I post this on your door?" He holds up a flier for a skateboard tournament—optimistic considering all the rain.

"Sure," I hear Annabelle say in a sugary voice.

I jerk my head around and see her smiling widely at the guy.

"So you skate?" she asks, like it's a fascinating pursuit, not just riding a board on wheels, which is boring when you think about it.

"Yeah, you should come watch the tournament. We get some good people."

"Great. We'll try to make it," I say loudly, to cover up whatever Annabelle is saying next to me. I ignore the sharp elbow she gives me. "So, yeah, go ahead and hang it on the door, and you can tell our next customer to come in."

I'm not sure there's anyone out there, but I want this clown gone. Something about him just rubs me the wrong way. Maybe it's the hair: it's trying too hard to be retro or slacker or Beatles mop-top…or something.

"Thanks, dude," he says, flashing me the peace sign.

"You didn't have to be rude," Annabelle says, after he leaves.

"What?" I ask, holding up my palms. "I told him he could put up his flier for his little skating fest."

Annabelle grumbles but doesn't have a chance to say anything because our next customer walks in: an African American girl with cornrows whom I've seen on the beach a few times, collecting shells in the rain.

"I hear you guys are a couple," the girl says bluntly, settling down across from us. "It's too cute that you're doing a matchmaking booth together." She twirls one of the ends of her cornrows around her finger as she smiles.

I purse my lips. "Actually, do you know Sarah Walker? We're—"

But before I can finish my sentence to set the record straight, Annabelle has a coughing fit, bending over and hacking her lungs out like she just inhaled noxious fumes.

"Sorry about that," Annabelle says a minute later, when she finally stops. She straightens and smiles. "Why don't you go ahead and fill out this form?"

I shoot Annabelle a look, but she ignores me. No problem. I can set the record straight another time. Besides,

I know what's really bothering Annabelle. It isn't hearing about Sarah; it's how she has lost her astrology mojo and I am the horoscope king of Gingerbread. You'd think this would prove to her once and for all that astrology is a joke. I mean, she's been studying it for years, and here I am, one-upping her left and right. What more proof could you need that it's a bunch of guesswork based on absolutely nothing?

But it's just made her more of a freak, studying it in her spare time and coming in with info that is more and more out there, like how retrograde planets impact the houses or whatever. If it weren't for the fact that I'm the one who's right all the time, it might even annoy me.

"You want to start?" I ask Annabelle. I try not to smirk.

"Yes," she says, biting the end of the word. After scanning the form, she glances up at the girl with a friendly smile. "Aisha, you're a Taurus, which means you can be stubborn. When you set your sights on something, you go for it with everything you've got."

Aisha is nodding.

"You have Venus in Aries which means you're fiery, and guys love that," Annabelle says. "You just have to choose one wisely."

"That's where it gets hard," Aisha states. "I've been choosing unwisely."

"And that's our specialty," Annabelle says. "With that fire you have, you need to seek out fire signs."

"You think?" I ask.

Annabelle shoots me a look of poison, but I've seen my opportunity and I'm taking it.

"Aisha's rising sign is Gemini." Aisha looks confused so I explain. "Your rising sign is like the mask you wear out in the world, the way you present yourself. But it covers your true self, which is more down to earth. Am I right?"

Aisha nods. "Yeah, I'm definitely a creature of habit. I have my set ways, and I stick to them."

I turn and give Annabelle a look that says, "Watch the master," and then I give Aisha all I've got. "You're attracted to signs like Aries or Sagittarius, and they like your Gemini shell, but the real you needs an earth boy, like a Virgo."

"What dates are Virgo?" she asks.

"August 22 to September 22," I say, and her eyes light up.

"The guy I'm totally crushing on at work has a birthday August 30!" she says.

Am I even surprised? The king does it again. Annabelle shoots me another withering glare, but Aisha is bubbling over.

"He's totally not the type I usually go for, but I keep noticing him even though my girlfriends say he's boring. But I say still waters run deep, you know?"

I nod. "Definitely."

Aisha reaches over the table and grabs my hands. "Thank you," she says, looking into my eyes. "I was making things hard on myself, doubting my own feelings, but now I know I need to trust my instincts and go for it."

"I couldn't agree more, Aisha."

"Oh, please!" cries Annabelle.

Aisha looks up, puzzled.

Annabelle blinks and then manages a shaky smile. "Sorry…I was just thinking about something else. I got distracted…"

"Well, I can see why everyone raves about this place," Aisha says as she stands up to leave. "The love you guys have for each other is contagious."

"Actually we're not together," Annabelle mutters, but it's too late. Aisha's gone. "I'd rather gouge out my eyes than be with Pete Riley," she says to the empty doorway. "Just for the record."

"Interesting," I add flatly, my eyes also on the door. "I'd rather become a monk than have an astrology freak as a girlfriend."

She's about to respond when Sarah marches in the door.

"Hey, can you cut out early today?" Sarah asks, not giving Annabelle so much as a glance or acknowledgment that she's present.

"Yes, absolutely," I say. The chair screeches as I push it away from the table.

Sarah makes a weird purring sound, running her fingers through my hair. It scratches, but I smile like I think it's the greatest feeling in the world.

Annabelle rolls her eyes.

"Should we go to the movies or shoot some pool?" Sarah asks, continuing to ignore Annabelle.

"Whatever you want," I say. It's becoming harder and harder to smile, but I keep my lips frozen in the upright and locked position.

Sarah leans against the table and looks at me from under her lashes. "So I've been thinking about my next tattoo," she murmurs.

Oh, please, no, not this again…

"I'm picturing how a tree would look right here," she says, pointing to the underside of her wrist. "Something stark, with no leaves, just the empty branches. Or do you think I should get something else?"

Her cells phone rings, and she flips it open just as Annabelle mumbles, "Why not get a ball and chain, since that's what you are?"

I bite my lip to keep from laughing out loud. The problem is: it isn't funny at all. Annabelle is totally right.

Vanessa Tarasov

Born July 18: Cancer ♋

Rising Sign: Capricorn ♑

You lead with your heart, which means you feel things deeply, for better and for worse. Your fear of getting hurt often has you keeping your feelings locked away. This summer, things may not go as you'd hoped. When this happens, don't be afraid to try a new way to tackle the obstacles blocking your path.

chapter 10

It's been a long afternoon after a long week after what is feeling like the longest summer ever. Every day seems to bring some new form of torture. Either it's Sarah, showing up unannounced to whisk Pete away, or it's Pete sitting here beside me, waxing poetic and wise with his horoscopes while I just sink lower and lower with mine.

"Thanks, this is fantastic," our second-to-last customer says. He's some wrinkled old geezer who must be close to retirement age. I suppose his look of genuine happiness should make me feel better...but it doesn't. He gets up and shuffles out, all excited to go out and find his perfect match based on Pete's unfailing astrological wisdom. Which seems to happen on a regular basis.

I've lost count of how many people have come in to tell us they found love, or at least a date, based on our advice. Pete's advice. Whatever. All I know is that I'm starting to feel like I've seen it all. I'm thirsty; the rain thunking on the tin roof is giving me a headache; and all I want is to be curled up at home drinking a cup of cocoa.

I'm staring at my flip-flops as the final customer slips into the chair across from us, so it's not until she speaks that I look up, shocked. It is none other than Vanessa, the bitter shrew herself.

"No way!" I say before I can stop myself.

Vanessa grins sheepishly. "Your booth is the talk of Gingerbread, so I had to see it for myself," she says. "And I just read this article in the *New York Times* about young entrepreneurs, so I figure this is my shot to see two of them in action."

"That would be us," I say, trying to muster some enthusiasm but falling flat as always. We *have* made a chunk of change this summer, not that money was the point. But it's not a bad side effect. It might be the only good one.

"Here's the form," Pete says, passing it to her.

She smirks as she takes a pen and fills it out. "All right, show me your magic," she says, hurriedly scribbling. "I want to see if there's any truth to the legend of the tiny booth that finds love for all." There's swagger in her tone, but she's tugging a little on a lock of hair, which she only does when she's nervous. Weird.

"You know me too well, so I want to hear what Pete has to say," she says.

I've whined to her for hours about losing my astrology mojo—and about Pete—so I'm not sure if I should give her a smile of thanks for letting me off the hook or ask what the hell it is she's really doing here. She's one of the only people who gets that Pete and I aren't an item anymore...isn't she?

"Thanks, Vanessa," Pete says in his "professional" voice, adding cryptically: "I'm glad we can move past whatever problems we had at the beginning of the summer." He peeks at her birth info, checks something in a book, and then folds his hands on the table in front of him.

"Here's your problem in the nutshell. You're a Capricorn rising, which means you present like a tough girl, but your true self is a Cancer. You're much more sensitive than people realize...maybe even more sensitive than you realize yourself."

I see Vanessa almost start to nod and then catch herself.

Pete leans back in the chair, wincing as the loose screw pokes him in the back. "You need to find a quiet, unaggressive type, like a Pisces or Libra."

It's not bad advice for a Cancer with a rising Capricorn, but Pete is off the mark for Vanessa. She's all about high-powered alpha males. I mean, Silas was a Yale-bound, hockey-playing, captain-of-the-debate team future CEO. That's just what Vanessa goes for. Or went for. Besides, it's not like the bitter shrew is really looking for love anyway.

"Does that make sense?" he asks.

Vanessa grins at me. "It does. And thanks! I like seeing what you guys are about." She stands up. "Call me later, Annabelle," she says as she heads out.

A moment later Sarah comes in. I check my watch and realize we need to close up. Pete kisses her. For several seconds. Ugh. I should have locked the door behind Vanessa. Sarah finally removes herself from Pete's jaw and treats me to a sugary smile. I brace myself. The few times she's bothered to notice I exist, it's always been to insult me—and very lamely, I might add.

"So did Pete tell you about our plans for the fall?" she asks.

Like I'd really care. Though I can't believe they're actually making plans for the fall.

"I'm going up to his place the first snow so we can ski. Then…"

The rest of her words are lost as my head starts spinning. If I weren't sitting down, I'd probably fall over. Pete ski willingly? That's never happened in the entire time I've known him. But he's just grinning—not saying that she's delusional but going along—like he skis for fun all the time and can't wait to get back on the slopes.

And that's when I feel like I've gotten a body blow. This whole time I've been thinking Pete is just with Sarah as a fling, but now I realize I had it all wrong. If he's making plans to see her in the fall, making plans to *ski* with her, then this really means something. Pete likes her, maybe more than he ever liked me. I *love* skiing. He knows that. But he never once brought up the possibility of doing it together, or even of my visiting him…

Pete likes Sarah.

I can't believe it, but the truth is right in front of me, as Sarah pulls him close for another kiss. I want to lie down on the floor and never get up.

"So you want me to put the books away?" Pete asks when the kiss ends.

"Um, you guys go ahead," I say, using every bit of strength I have to sound normal. "I'll clean up here."

"Thanks," Pete says.

I watch as the happy couple strolls off. At least they're strolling into the rain, not the sunset. After they go, part of me wants to cry for a while, but I don't give in to that. This is the summer after my junior year, one of the most important summers of my life, and I'm letting it slip by, wasting it thinking about a guy who's totally into someone else. It's time to get this summer started right, and I know exactly what that means.

I sit down at the table and pick up my favorite of all the books: *The Star Path to Love*. I'm going to find my own summer love, or at least a fun fling who will hold my hand on the Ferris wheel and kiss me good night at the door and not freak out like a lunatic if I mention a planet being in retrograde. With a little help from the stars, I'll find the perfect guy in no time and salvage this disaster of a summer.

I know he's out there.

• • •

The Teen Boardwalk Dances are so awful they're fun. They're held every Thursday in the Gingerbread Beach Recreation Hall, a building that should have been condemned in the 1960s, with a leaky roof and uneven floors from years of water damage…not to mention the endless supply of stale cookies served by the hostile owner, Mr. Heller.

The music is even worse. Mr. Heller uses the dances as opportunities to float down memory lane, dipping into CDs from his youth, treating us to lots of eighties pop and the occasional Led Zeppelin medley. True, it is good music but not exactly danceable. But hey, what can you expect for five bucks and free refills on punch? Quite watery punch, I might add.

But this is where I'm beginning my quest for the perfect summer guy. If the stars have anything to do with it, I think I'm going to leave here happy. My daily horoscope advised taking a risk tonight, and I have Venus in Cancer, which means I am very receptive to love. Okay, it also means I might have a tendency to see romance where it doesn't exist, but I'm too clearheaded to fall into that trap.

When I walk in, the place is packed with people dancing, crowds around the punch and cookie table, and couples making out against the walls. I see Pete and Sarah on the edge of the dance floor and look away. No time to dwell on them, not when love awaits. Or at least fun summer romance.

I ease over to the edge of the dance floor, not too far from the refreshment table, so I can scope out the room and also be scoped. I'm wearing a light-blue halter dress and sparkly ballet flats, and I took the time to flat iron my hair. Unfortunately, the second I walked into the humid drizzle it frizzed up, but it's back in barrettes so at least it's contained. And I'm wearing makeup, which I almost never bother with. But a special night calls for real effort, so I put in my time with the mascara wand. I even brought supplies for touch-ups in the little black bag Grandma Hillary brought me from Paris last year.

On my very first inspection of the room, I see a promising candidate. He's not a regular; he's got sandy-colored hair and one of those round faces that has boyish charm. Plus he's tall, which I like...and—best of all—he's wearing a Yankees jersey. *Score!* I shoot Pete a quick glare without realizing it but then focus. I try to catch the guy's eye, and when I finally do, I smile flirtatiously. Or maybe not. No? Maybe I somehow leered at him because he looks away fast and then heads out the door.

Nice. I've succeeded in scaring him off. Not the start I was hoping for.

"Hey, Annabelle," a guy says. It takes me a minute to recognize John, one of our very first Star Shack customers—the tall college dude with the messy black hair and horn-rimmed glasses.

"How's it going?" I ask.

"Oh, you know, 'looking for love in all the wrong places,'" he says, smiling like he's told a joke. Which I totally don't get. I guess he can tell because he explains, "Yeah, you just got here. It was the first song Mr. Heller played."

"Someone wrote a song called 'Looking for Love in All the Wrong Places?'" I ask. "Could it get more cheesy?"

"Actually, yes," he says. "It was a country song."

We both laugh. I give John a quick once-over to see if he might have summer romance possibility. But he was a customer, and I don't want to be unprofessional. Plus he's cute but in a soft, almost nerdy way, which isn't really my type.

"Well, I'm off to find a Scorpio or Cancer who wants to save the world," he says, and he disappears into the crowd.

I scan the room again...my eyes zeroing in on a guy with long brown hair in a ponytail. Normally long hair doesn't really do it for me, but he's laughing at something his friend is saying, which makes him seem nice, and he has sharp cheekbones, which is one of my weaknesses. Pete has great cheekbones. Not that I'll be thinking about him tonight. No. He's the past, and tonight I am all about my present and future. Right.

I smile at ponytail guy, and he grins back, widely. This is good. Then suddenly a hand appears on his shoulder. A hand with bright pink nails attached to a girl who is giving me a very hostile look. Oops. Not so good.

I turn away quickly, pretend to straighten my bag, and then notice a different guy in the corner looking at me. He's stocky and bookish but tall with decent cheekbones. And he saw me first, which means he's single and interested. Now things are happening. I smile at him, and he waves a little and then starts making his way across the dance floor toward me. I get a tingly feeling of anticipation that makes my face flush and my heart beat just a little faster. Finally!

But as he steps out from the crush of bodies swaying to "I Can't Fight This Feeling," a shiver of revulsion runs down my spine. This is no guy; this is a man. An *old* man. He's got to be at least forty. How creepy is it that he's here at a teen dance?

"Want to dance?" he asks.

"No thanks," I say, folding my arms over my chest and turning away.

"Come on," he presses. "I saw you checking me out."

Eww. "I didn't realize you were old enough to be my dad," I tell him frostily and am satisfied to see him turn red. "I think I need glasses."

He stalks off, and a couple on the dance floor catches my eye. It's Pete and Sarah. Her claws are wrapped around his shoulders, and I feel my lips turn down in disgust. He's dressed up tonight…he's wearing a button-down Oxford shirt with the sleeves rolled up. He never used to dress up for me. Why is he with her? It just makes no sense. He catches sight of me and almost seems to pull Sarah closer. I turn away to avoid making the universal sign for *barf.*

"Excuse me, would you like to dance?"

I nearly jump. The guy in front of me has appeared out of nowhere. He's like a magical gift: totally hot, with honey-blond hair, killer cheekbones, and a tight black T-shirt that shows off very toned arms. And most important, he is clearly not over eighteen.

"I'd love to," I say, smiling.

He takes my hand and leads me to the dance floor, then pulls me close. This is good. I see Pete over Cute Guy's shoulder, and he rolls his eyes, turning away. Even better. I wrap my arms around Cute Guy and sway to the music.

"Want to go out for some air?" he asks after two dances.

"Sure," I say. It's stuffy in here. But frankly, I'm ready to get to know the guy who's going to be my summer romance. And to get away from Pete and Tattoo Girl.

We walk out to the falling-down deck behind the rec center. A few other couples are huddled there, but he leads me around the back wall to a quiet corner where we have complete privacy.

"I'm Nate," he says.

"Annabelle," I say, reaching out my hand.

He smiles, shakes it, and then pulls me close and mashes his face on mine. *What the—?* I squirm away. "Whoa, slow down!" I say, hoping to sound playful but coming out a little shrill. But really, he just practically mauled me. I wipe my lips.

"Oh, you're one of those," he says.

"One of what?" I ask, hands on my hips.

"A tease," he says.

"Because I danced with you? And wanted to talk?"

He grins. "No one goes outside just to *talk*," he says, as if I'm an idiot.

"Civilized people do," I snap. The breeze from the ocean is chilly, and I wrap my arms around myself.

He snorts. "Right, keep telling yourself that," he says. He deliberately brushes against me as he moves by to go back to the dance.

And then I'm alone. I lean against the side of the rec hall, even though the wood is damp and goose bumps are forming on my arms and legs. Talk about a perfect night! I repel one guy, insult another guy's girlfriend, get hit on by a pedophile, and then get called a tease.

I reach into my bag for my cell phone to call Vanessa. Maybe I can salvage what's left of the evening in front of her TV, watching movies, eating junk food, and dissing guys. I am so in the mood for the camaraderie of the bitter shrew.

But as my fingers touch my phone I realize my bag is suspiciously empty. My heart drops as I take everything out. My heart pounds. *Oh my God*...that jerk. He stole my wallet. Nate didn't just slobber all over me and insult me, he ripped me off too. Unreal! Have I really fallen this low? I creep down the stairs avoiding eye contact with anyone.

I pause at the bottom of the steps, debating whether to go back in there and cause a scene. But really…what will happen? Nate will deny it; I'll look like a lunatic. No, best just to go home, cancel all my credit cards, and deal later with pressing charges (if that's what I even want to do). There will be no movies or chatting with Vanessa tonight. Nope…there will be nothing but more misery.

I head home in the rain, not caring that I'm getting soaked. What does it matter? Honestly, if I catch pneumonia, it'll be a good thing. At least I'll have an excuse not to show up at the Star Shack tomorrow.

Charlie Fisher

Born September 12: Virgo (not happy to be called a Virgin) ♍

Rising Sign: Pisces ♓

You seek perfection in all aspects of your life, but your practicality keeps you grounded. Sometimes your urge to fix things can annoy those around you, but the right person will find your ability to problem solve an asset. This summer, your stubborn side will emerge, but don't worry: when the time comes, you won't let it get in the way of doing the right thing.

chapter 11

Have a good day!" my mom calls as I head out into the rain. "Say hi to Annabelle!"

"Thanks," I say, rubbing my eyes. I decide not to remind Mom that I'm barely talking to Annabelle. There isn't much of a point. Anyway, I'm too wiped out to talk. I'm going to need ten cups of coffee just to stay awake today. I was up half the night after the dance. I wish I could say I was thinking about the magical night I had with Sarah, but honestly? I was never so glad to have a date end.

No, what kept me sleepless until four in the morning was the memory of Annabelle in the arms of that sleazy guy with the cheesy black T-shirt.

Problem 1: He was all over her on the dance floor.

Problem 2: They headed out to the back deck. Everyone knows what happens out on the back deck.

Problem 3: This would seem to mean that Annabelle has suddenly become an easy, free-wheeling party girl.

Problem 4: They never came back.

So I have no idea if they talked all night, if he walked her home, or if she let him kiss her…or what. I kept tossing and turning, my mind racing through a million horrible scenarios. I mean, Annabelle and I aren't together, but we're still friends, and you worry when your friends fall for jerks. Sure, I don't want to date her or anything, but I don't want to see her get hurt or taken advantage of either. And guys like that specialize in doing damage. You could just tell by looking at him.

Of course, it didn't help that Sarah saw me staring at them on the dance floor and got all worked up, saying I was there with her, not Annabelle. Which you'd think was obvious. I tried to explain that I was worried about my business partner, but Sarah thought that guy looked perfectly nice. Actually her exact words were "Boring, like your little friend." Yes. Very insightful.

Sarah was still in a huff when we left, and it took a lot of work to calm her down and get her out of my car. I had to promise to see a chick flick at the movies tonight. I was honestly willing to promise anything to finally be alone. Though I'll regret it tonight when I'm stuck watching a stupid musical montage of love scenes with Sarah falling all over me.

I swing by the Opera Café. I don't know why I bother; I can barely even get a cup of coffee because Daisy is there and Jed can't seem to function when he's with his new girlfriend. He's too busy holding her hand or crooning opera to her to do something like, say, serve coffee. I finally get to the Star Shack with my house blend just as the rain lulls. Annabelle is already there.

"Hey," I say, walking in and sitting down on the chair with the loose screw, the consequence of being the second one to arrive.

She nods but doesn't speak. I'm a little surprised. I thought she'd be going on and on about her date, rubbing it in my face that she was with some guy. But whatever… it's not like I want to hear about it. Plus we'll probably just fight when I tell her I think the guy is trouble.

I sip my coffee as Annabelle stares down at her hands. Not that we usually chat up a storm in the mornings, but we still at least occasionally trash talk about baseball…and the Yankees did win last night. Maybe her night wasn't so great after all. But I'm not asking. It's not like I'm interested.

"My mom says hi," I finally tell her, just to break the silence.

She doesn't answer. She just stares at the pile of astrology books on the table.

"So, good night last night?" I ask. Okay, so maybe I'm a little interested. And really I should give her my advice before we start getting customers.

"Fine," Annabelle answers, not looking up. Her voice is hoarse and tight.

She definitely doesn't want to talk about it. No big deal. I flip through *Astrology and You: Perfect Together*, but I can't focus on any of the words…I'm way too distracted by how quiet Annabelle is. I steal a quick peek at her and notice she has circles under her eyes, like she hasn't slept well either. I'm about to ask what's going on when she suddenly raises her hands to her face.

"Hey, are you okay?" I ask.

She shakes her head, and I realize she's crying.

"What is it? What's wrong?" My arm goes around her automatically.

But she shakes me off and doesn't answer, just roots around in her bag for a tissue to blow her nose. All at once, a flash of worry hits me. Did that creep do something to her? If he did, I'll kill him.

"I'm sorry; I'm sorry…I'm fine," she chokes out, pulling out another tissue to wipe the tears off her face. She sniffs and forces an empty smile. "Let's open the door and get started."

"But—"

"Really, let's just get started."

I'm not refusing her when she looks this miserable. I'm even less happy when I open the door and let in our first customer—a frat boy type who looks suspiciously like he'd be great friends with Creepy Black T-Shirt Dude.

He fills out his form and hands it to us. I am sneaking looks at Annabelle, with worry consuming me. She's pale, practically trembling.

"Pete, you want to start?" Annabelle asks.

I grab the clipboard. "Let's see, September 12...you're a Virgo." I feel as if I'm on autopilot; I hardly know what I'm saying. "The overriding trait of Virgins is—"

"Whoa, who are you calling a virgin?" the guy asks.

"Sorry..." I glance at his name. "Charlie. It's just the name of the sign, not a comment on your status."

"Okay," he says, looking at me skeptically.

"Here, let me handle this one," Annabelle says.

The guy's face lights up, which would normally annoy me, but it's clear that she needs a distraction. While she listens to him start to ramble, an insane idea hits me. I ease open the copy of *A Year of Horoscopes* and look up Annabelle's birthday. If this astrology thing comes so easy to me, why not trust it? It takes me half the morning to piece things together from a few books—we have a good flow of people coming in and out, and Annabelle loses herself in giving them advice—but if the stars are right, I start to get a picture of what is going on. Annabelle was in prime position to be duped last night, ready to see romantic possibility in a person with very different motives. So now my question is: what was this guy after?

My stomach growls, breaking my train of thought. Normally Annabelle would make a joke or at least roll her eyes, but today she doesn't seem to even notice. She also hasn't noticed how I've kept my mouth shut and let her handle all the advice. This is bad. But I can't figure it out on an empty stomach.

"I'm starving," I say, stretching a little. "How about I get us some sandwiches from the deli?"

"Okay," Annabelle says, reaching for her backpack. "Let me just give you...oh." Her face falls, and she drops her backpack.

"What, did you forget your wallet? No problem. I can loan you money. Or we can just take it from the Star Shack stash." So far we've just let the money pile up in a manila envelope in a drawer. We might as well start using it.

Annabelle shakes her head. "Actually I'm not hungry."

"It's no big deal if you don't have money," I insist. "You can pay me back if you don't want to use Star Shack money."

I'm shocked to see tears pool in her eyes. "Really, I'm not hungry. Just go and get yourself something."

Clearly she wants to be left alone. I can take the hint, so I head to the deli trying to put it all together. Did she just forget her wallet? That's not something to cry about; it has to be more. There was something in her eyes, almost as if she were ashamed. Did she *lose* her wallet? But if so, why not just admit it? And that wouldn't have her feeling embarrassed. Everyone loses stuff. I'm worse than she is.

I order a turkey and Swiss on rye and think back about what I've read. If I'm going to take this star stuff seriously, just for a second, I'll assume that I know that Annabelle's in a place where she'll be easily fooled, where someone might try to take advantage of her. And there was also something about watching out for the things close to you. Could that mean something material, like a wallet?

And then something completely insane occurs to me.

Is it possible that Creepy Black T-Shirt Dude *stole* her wallet? It can't be, right, though…can it? I mean, no one would stoop that low. Would they? It would be stupid, because he'd get caught too. But it would explain why neither of them returned to the dance. And weirdly enough, a part of me is relieved at that scenario.

I wait until Annabelle takes an afternoon bathroom break and then peek in her backpack. I don't want to violate her privacy or anything, but I have to know. Sure enough, she has a book, some loose change, and a receipt from the grocery store that's a few days old. The pocket where she normally keeps her wallet is empty.

So now I'm almost certain. Ten-to-one that jackass stole her wallet. And if I have anything to say about it, he's going to pay.

• • •

It doesn't take much asking around to find out that his name is Nate Browning. Jed's served coffee to him (in between smooching with Daisy) and says he's been here for about a week now. I jog home to Google his address. On the way, Sarah calls. *Uh-oh.* I forgot our chick-flick date.

"Hey, I'm really sorry, but I can't make it tonight," I tell her in one breath, flipping my phone open. I know it's best to get this done fast.

"What?" she practically screeches.

"Hey, it's just a movie," I tell her. "We can do it another time."

"I spent two hours shopping for the perfect dress," she huffs.

Who buys a new dress to go sit in the dark for two hours? I wonder, but mutter: "Sorry." I open the front door of my house and kick off my wet sneakers.

"You better make it up to me," she says.

"Sure," I say, already hanging up. "Bye!"

Once again, I feel a very odd wash of relief, in spite of what I'm about to do.

• • •

Nate's not home, and his mom isn't sure where he is. I check all the spots on the boardwalk and finally find him at Kitty's Clam Shack sitting with a group of guys as moronic looking as he is.

"Hey, Nate," I say, leaning over the table. "Can I have a word?"

"Who are you?" he asks in a hostile voice.

"We have some business," I say.

"I'm not sure I'm interested," he says, and his meathead buddies laugh.

"Trust me, you are," I say.

If I have to go into it in front of his friends I will, but I'd much rather get him alone. It'll go easier that way. He gives me a long scowling look and then stands up and follows me out of Kitty's into the cool drizzle outside.

"So what's this about?" he asks, folding his arms over his beefed-up chest. He looks like he shoots up steroids. Which, come to think of it, is probably why he's sunk as low as stealing wallets from girls. Unless I'm completely wrong. I mean, do I really trust the stars?

I take a deep breath and go for it. If I'm wrong, I'm wrong. Worst-case scenario: I'll piss this guy off and apologize. And hope that he doesn't take a swing at me. "You have something that belongs to a friend of mine, and I need it back," I hear myself say, very evenly.

He holds up his hands. "Dude, I don't know what you're talking about." He takes a step back toward the door.

I move close to him, right up in his face. He may do the gym thing, but baseball gives you real muscle and I'm pretty sure I can take him if it comes to that. But I don't want it to come to that. I've never been in a fight before. Plus, I know myself: I'm so pissed at what he did to Annabelle I'm going to go from zero to a hundred if he gets physical and probably end up hurting myself even more than I'd hurt him. I can hear my beating heart in my ears.

"You have Annabelle Lomax's wallet, and I need it back, with everything still inside."

He stares at me for a second, I guess trying to gauge how far I'm willing to go. And he must see something in my eyes because he looks away fast.

"Sure, dude, whatever," he says. "I was going to give it back to her. I just wanted to teach her a lesson."

The shock that I was actually right—that the *stars* were right, and that I read them correctly, no faking—is outweighed only by the shock of the garbage coming out of this guy's mouth. "You wanted to teach her a lesson," I repeat.

"I was just pissed she wouldn't mess around, you know?"

"No, I don't know," I say. Unconsciously, my fists clench at my sides. My jaw twitches. I try to take a deep breath.

"Relax. I didn't know she was your girlfriend," he says, backing away.

"She's not my girlfriend," I say.

"Well, she's obviously something if you're this amped up," he mumbles. "The wallet's back at my mom's place."

I ignore his statement about Annabelle. "Well then, let's go get it. And you might want to put an extra twenty in there, just so she's knows you're really sorry."

Nate groans.

"Because you *are* sorry, right?" I ask menacingly.

He nods. "Yeah, I'm sorry I ever agreed to come to this deadbeat town. I'm calling my dad and getting out of here first thing tomorrow."

I slap him on the back as we reach my car. "Nate, that's the smartest thing you've said all night."

• • •

Twenty minutes later, I'm stopped at a light, the rain hammering down on the roof of my car, Iggy Pop howling from the speakers about a girl named Candy that he lost twenty years ago…and best of all, Annabelle's wallet on the seat next to me. On the corner, I see Aisha and the guy she got together with, the one she decided to ask out after coming to the Star Shack. She dropped by yesterday just to thank us again, to tell us how well it's been going and how perfect he is for her.

They're under a big yellow umbrella, and he has his arm around her. Just as the light turns green, he leans down and kisses her cheek. My lips curl in a brief smile, but then it fades. Someone behind me honks, and I step on the gas.

I think about how happy they look, how happy Jed looks with Daisy. Honestly, I can't walk down the boardwalk without bumping into at least one couple that got together after a reading at the Star Shack. I think about tonight, about how I was able to figure out why Annabelle was upset about Nate.

All of this came from astrology.

As I turn left on Magnolia Street, I make myself say the words that I've been scared even to think, ever since Nate and I parted ways. (He told his mom he was "returning a friend's wallet." Classic.)

"It's not a coincidence," I whisper out loud.

I mean, giving good advice once or twice can happen to anyone. But I've been doing it consistently for weeks now. Annabelle has aced her fantasy league every year since she was fourteen, a league with grown men and women who spend half their waking lives analyzing stats. Again, could it just be random luck?

If I'm willing to take the crazy risk I took this morning, to go out on a wild limb, I can make myself believe it.

Maybe, just maybe, there is something to this science of the stars.

Just then, the smile comes back to my face. And this time it won't go away. Because if there is something to astrology…hey. I'm pretty damn good at it.

Ana Sanchez

Born August 13: Leo ♌

Rising Sign: Gemini ♊

You look for deeper meaning in the world around you and accept nothing less than the truth. Friends love your fun-loving nature, but romantic interests in your life burn bright and flair out fast. This summer, keep one thing in mind: once you truly hit rock bottom, there's no place to go but up.

chapter 12

Mornings in Gingerbread I used to wake up to the cozy sound of rain on the roof, the faint smell of the ocean in the moist air, and anticipation bubbling as I thought about all the lazy, wonderful things I would do in the day ahead.

But this morning? The rain thuds mercilessly, making my head hurt; the humid air smells like the eggs my mom burned; and thinking about the day ahead turns my stomach into an acidic mess. I thought the worst was when Pete left me on the boardwalk to run off with Cool Tattoo Girl.

Nope: I was wrong. It turns out the worst came in the form of finding out that Pete genuinely *cares* for Sarah, topped off with getting my pocket picked by the only guy willing to dance with me. Is there a status worse than loser status? If so, I'm about a zillion rungs below it.

My alarm beeps at me, and I hit snooze for the fifth time. Summers past I didn't even need an alarm clock, but I had to take the one out of Gabe's room so that I'd be up in time to get to the Star Shack. I could see sleeping through the whole day. I would prefer it, in fact.

Do I really have to go in today? Am I really even necessary? Pete gives much better advice than I do. Everyone knows it. I suppose my one consolation is that Pete has no idea what happened with Nate. If he knew, I'd be on an airplane to meet Gabe and Grandma Hillary in Central Asia in a heartbeat. I'm not even sure what country they're in now, since I haven't heard from either of them in a week, but it wouldn't matter—I'd rather be on my own in a foreign country where people eat horse than stuck in Gingerbread with my humiliation known.

But best just to stick with the routine. When all is said and done, this is a dare, and I'm...winning? Right: winning.

I grab my pillow, hurl it across the room, and stomp out of bed.

• • •

I usually make it a point to open the Star Shack early so I can at least claim the good chair—so I'm surprised to see Pete there when I arrive. Make that Pete and Sarah. *Ugh.* They don't even notice me as I approach the door.

"I'm just asking where you were last night," Sarah snaps. Her back is to me, and she has her hands on her hips. I guess there's trouble in paradise. For the first time since the Nate fiasco, I smile. But then I feel mean and then self-pitying...and then just sort of numb.

"Just doing some stuff at home," Pete says.

"I called your house, and your mom said you were out," Sarah says. "Were you with *her*?"

I wonder who *her* is. I'd think it was me, but there's zero reason for Sarah to be threatened by my pathetic friendship with Pete (actually, that's too generous a term—I think "awkward business nonpartnership" comes closer), and I'm sure she's figured that out by now. She may be bitchy and annoying, but she's not stupid. Which begs the question: Is Pete seeing someone else too? What's *happened* to him? Has Star Shack fame gone to his head?

Pete spies me in the doorway over Sarah's shoulder. "Hey," he says weakly.

"Hey."

Sarah turns to face me, and her eyes narrow. Odd: She acts like I'm interrupting her and I don't belong, but isn't this where I work? Yes. Yes, it is. I rented it. I'm the one who's supposed to be here. She is not. I glance back at Pete and see that he's already slumped in the good chair, face obscured by an astrology book. Books are stacked in front of him and—*wait a second.* The one he's holding is a new one: *Signs of Love.* Did Pete *buy* that? No, that can't be possible.

"What are you reading?" Sarah asks, disdain in her voice.

"Just boning up on energies and qualities of the signs," he says nonchalantly from behind the starry purple cover.

I blink. The world—which has never seemed like a very

sane place this summer—suddenly flips into pure surreal dreamland. Pete is talking the astrology talk as if he's a seasoned pro, like one of those online chat hosts I am sad to admit I tune into sometimes.

"Oh, and Annabelle?" he says, before I can grill him on his choice of reading material. "Your wallet is in the drawer."

I sit down before my legs collapse out from under me. "My *what*?" I ask.

Sarah gives me an I-must-be-mentally-impaired look. (Which isn't too far off the mark.) "He said your wallet," she mutters. "You must have left it somewhere."

Well, I guess you could say that. I mean, it was *somewhere*, but that somewhere was Nate's slimy paws. So how on earth did Pete get his hands on it? Maybe it's not my wallet. But when I open the drawer, I see that it is.

All right, the world *has* turned to surreal dreamland. Because everything in my wallet seems to be intact. Wait, more than everything—I didn't have this much money. There's a crisp twenty-dollar bill inside. What the hell is going on? Did Nate not steal my wallet? I am very, very confused.

"So we saw you at the dance the other night," Sarah says, smiling at me, though her eyes are ice cold. "That guy sure seemed into you."

"Um, I don't know," I say. Boy, do I not want to talk about this. And why isn't she taking the hint to leave?

Pete has never, ever seemed so into a book in his life, even his favorites.

"He was cute," she continues.

I shrug, unable to fake any kind of answer.

"What's his name?" she asks.

"Nate." Just saying it brings back the grossness of his slimy mouth on mine and the sick humiliation he left me with.

"Are you going to see him again?" she asks.

I don't even get why she cares, but Pete finally looks up.

"Nate had to leave town," he says evenly.

Sarah and I both stare at him.

"How do you know?" she asks.

Pete shrugs and puts the book down, marking his page with the flap. "I ran into him the other night. We had some...business. But it's over, and he mentioned he was leaving today."

"Business?" Sarah barks, for once her mind in total sync with mine.

"Yeah, business?" I echo feebly. "Like what? Are you guys going to open an umbrella stand together or something?"

Pete laughs in spite of himself, and for a second I feel a warm rush. "Why is it that nobody has ever thought to open an umbrella stand on the Gingerbread Beach boardwalk?" he asks, glancing between Sarah and me. He picks up the book again. "By the way, A-Belle, the Yankees got creamed last night. But bad guys always end up getting their due…you know what I mean?"

He emphasizes the last five words—and then it hits me: he's the one who got my wallet back from Nate. I can't fathom how, but he must have found out Nate stole it. That's something the old Pete would have done, the one who cared about me. And suddenly it's like the sun coming out after a long, cold winter. I realize I'm smiling again, and my insides feel light and sweet as cotton candy. Is it possible…?

"I need to go," Sarah announces in a very loud voice. She yanks the book away from Pete's face and plants a sloppy kiss on his lips. His arms wrap around her, and I look away fast, the sun back under heavy clouds and the cotton candy squashed. Clearly I let a door open that obviously belongs closed.

They whisper for a moment, then she leaves, and our first customer of the day bounces in—some blond, bubble-eyed girl I've never seen in my life, who is wearing pigtails and looks vaguely like she stepped out of a modern adaptation of some '70s period piece. "You guys hooked up my best friend Aisha, and now it's my turn," she says happily. "I'm so ready for love!"

It's all I can do not to puke all over our book collection.

• • •

At around noon—after the usual Pete Riley Star Shack Love Fest—I realize I'm not going to make it to the end of the day without more caffeine. It's been nonstop after Twiggy (I can't remember that first blond's real name because I've been so distracted after the wallet thing), and I need a rest.

"Your most compatible matches are fire signs," Pete is saying. He's finishing up with a pretty, though heavily made-up, Hispanic girl. She has a sassy smile and will probably find a boyfriend the second she steps out of here. Oh, right—but that seems to happen to everyone who sets foot in the Star Shack. Everyone but me.

"Oh my God, you totally saved my summer!" she says, standing up and setting a ten-dollar bill on the table. "Thanks! My name's Ana, by the way. Ana Sanchez."

"Nice to meet you, Ana." Pete gives his salesman smile. He's been nauseatingly cheerful all day. "Just remember. What seems hopeless isn't. Leos get an unfairly bad rap. Mick Jagger is a Leo, which might explain it."

"Who?" the girl asks.

"He pitches for the Red Sox," I snap.

Pete bursts out laughing and then stops. "Um...he's actually the singer for the Rolling Stones. But he's played many of the same stadiums."

The girl shoots us both a quizzical look and heads out.

"Do you mind if I make a quick coffee run?" I ask Pete before he can say anything. I've barely looked at him since the kiss with Sarah.

"No problem. And do you mind if I leave a little early?"

So you can get ready for your hot date with Sarah tonight? Maybe you'll get matching tattoos. How precious. "Sure," I say.

"Hey, A-Belle—"

"What?" I am annoyed that he's using the nickname he gave me when he was twelve and abandoned when he was thirteen. I'm annoyed about a lot of things.

"Nothing." He picks up *Signs of Love.* He must have bought it, but now is not the time to ask. "The Leo thing wasn't meant as an insult," he adds.

"I didn't think it was." I leave before he can ask me to get him coffee. I know I'm being silly. He got my wallet from a scumbag. But how? Or am I completely wrong? But I know I'm not, so if anything, I should be grateful. More than grateful. But those few precious seconds where I thought he might still care for me made me realize how not over him I am. And his big make-out with Sarah made it obvious how totally over me he is. So—wait, what, oh, my God, what am I seeing?

I stagger backward a step.

Vanessa, the bitter shrew, the girl who mocks love like it's yesterday's boot-cut jeans…is kissing a tall guy. Forget tall—*kissing a guy!* Any guy. The fact that her lips are locked with a male human being confirms full Surreal Dreamland status. Have the end times arrived?

They are in front of Freddy's Fabulous, the pink neon of the funnel cake sign bathing them in soft light. When she comes up for breath, she sees me. The guy turns. I get my second shock of the afternoon: it's John with the horn-rimmed glasses—our customer seeking an idealistic Cancer. Which he has apparently found in the shape of my formerly cynical friend.

Vanessa rushes over to me, a goofy grin on her face. If there's one person who doesn't do goofy, it's Vanessa.

"Can you believe it?" she squeals in a whisper.

"No," I say. "I absolutely cannot believe it. What happened to the bitter shrew? And the summer without guys?"

She waves a hand like she's dismissing a silly fad. "I was angry and hurt, you know? Really it was just like Pete said. I was dating the wrong kind of guy. I needed someone who could appreciate my idealistic, sensitive side, you know?"

I am stuck back on the part where she says Pete was right. "Um, I guess."

"Pete said I needed to open my heart again, and he was right. And just when I was ready, I met John." Her voice gets all gooey when she says his name.

"How did it happen?" I ask, wondering why she hasn't mentioned the *New York Times* once during this entire conversation.

"It was at Putt a Little," she says, stars in her eyes, like meeting over mini golf is the most romantic thing ever. (Which, in all fairness, I suppose it could be.) "I was at that hole with the windmill. I gave my swing a little extra power because my club went flying and hit John back at the hole with the waterfall. I was so worried I'd hurt him, but he just started telling me about this article he'd read in the *New York Times* about head injuries that of course I'd read too. He actually quoted from it!"

A smile forms on my lips. For a second, I forget all the anger and bitterness. "Go on," I say.

"Well…that's when I knew it was meant to be. When we both knew."

I laugh. "Yeah, it looks like it," I say, and I squeeze her arm. I'm also completely stunned, but she doesn't need to know that. She practically skips back to John, who wraps her in his arms as if she's been off at sea for years—not chatting with a friend for less than two minutes. And that's when I realize the other thing I'm feeling: straight-up jealousy.

I want what she has. And not just with a summer fling. I want it with my best friend, the guy I know I'm meant to be with, despite everything that's happened. The guy who's proved love right, again and again.

• • •

The rain is really coming down as I start closing up shop. Pete is long gone, headed out a few minutes ago with an inscrutable "Bye," smiley as ever on his way to meet Sarah. We never talked about the wallet; we never talked about anything. We haven't talked about anything all summer long. We've talked *at* each other; we've talked *about* each other; we just haven't talked *to* each other.

"Hey, Annabelle," a voice says, making me jump. I turn and see Vanessa.

She smiles. "I just wanted to thank you and Pete again."

"You're welcome," I say, pretending to be busy as I neaten the stack of astrology books on the table, with *Signs of Love* on top—yet another thing I didn't talk about with Pete.

She nods, smiling dreamily. "Yeah. So you must be getting psyched about your birthday," she says, and her words stop me cold. The summer has been so miserable I'd actually forgotten about it. But August eighteenth is less than two weeks away.

It used to be the best day of the summer, of course. Pete and I would celebrate together with laser tag when I turned thirteen, a big carnival day when I turned fourteen, an all-day boating trip when I turned fifteen, and last year, sixteen, was the magical dinner at the resort followed by our first kiss. Perfection.

And look at me now.

Vanessa is staring at me, concern on her face. "You have plans, right?"

Normally, by now I'd be begging Pete to tell me what he'd cooked up. The ugly reality is that I'm clearly looking at the worst birthday of my life. Which I guess makes sense since this is the worst summer of my life.

"Um, yeah," I say. I can't admit the truth.

"Great," she says, cheerful again. "Well, I'm meeting John for dinner. He's taking me to the new all-you-can-eat raw bar at Kitty's."

"Sounds fun."

"See you later! Let me know about your birthday!"

I am finally alone.

I sit down in the good chair and put my face in my hands. Then I look around the Star Shack at the posters I hung so carefully, the signs I made, the forms I printed up, and the pile of astrology books. What was I thinking when I strong-armed Pete into the dare? Did I honestly believe it would help me get him back?

It is such a joke. The Star Shack has brought romance into the lives of so many friends and strangers I've lost count. It even softened the heart of the bitter shrew. This place has brought joy to legions, yet for me it's brought only one thing: complete misery.

I walk out, not bothering to straighten up or even lock the door. What do I care if the place gets broken into? I'd just as soon never set foot in it again. I continue home, barely seeing anything around me, the rain cold on my body. I will spend this night alone, just like last night, just like tomorrow night, and just like my birthday. I don't know exactly when things started to unravel, leaving me in this void, but I do know this: I am counting the days until we leave Gingerbread. I am never coming back again.

Jason Morrison

Born April 3: Aries ♈

Rising Sign: Taurus ♉

Your stubborn nature irritates some, but your solid determination often brings you the rewards you seek, especially in love. Those around you celebrate your enthusiasm and zest for life. This summer, take stock of yourself. You have a gift; don't be afraid to use it.

chapter 13

The phase of the moon at the exact time of your birth can give a whole other layer of meaning to the interpretation of your birth chart.

Wow, that sounds intense. My copy of *Astrology for the Serious Star Searcher* is well worth the money for gems like this. Though as I read further, I realize it takes a professional to figure it out since it depends on the number of degrees between the sun and the earth. I wonder if I could figure it out on my own if I read more about it—but most of these books discourage "lesser people" from trying the hard stuff. Well, screw it: so do baseball coaches.

My phone vibrates with a text that I don't bother reading. *Sarah.* There's no way I'm going to spend the night hearing about how she's going to decorate her college dorm room. Her new obsessive conversation piece is almost as boring as the senior prom conversation, but less mind numbing than the tattoo one.

Holy crap. This is where I am: rating my girlfriend's conversation on degrees of boring. Honestly, she can't find my talking about baseball and astrology very interesting, can she? The passage gets me thinking about a customer yesterday who had some unusual traits for a Pisces—which could be explained by this moon-phase thing—but then the phone vibrates again, snapping my concentration. I reach over and turn it off. There's no one I need to talk to tonight. I just want to get into this book so I can be even more on target at the Star Shack tomorrow.

The whole thing with Nate has me realizing a few things. I have an agenda now, an agenda that starts with becoming an astrology expert.

• • •

"If we had more time, we could get into nodes of the moon at the time of your birth," I say to the twenty-something slacker tourist who is getting up from the customer chair. "But I think you've got what you need to score a date."

He reaches over to fist bump me—nothing like a good astrology reading to make guys bond. "Thanks, brother," he says as he heads out. "Name's Jason, by the way. Jason Morrison. Like the lead singer of the Doors."

I try to smile. Wasn't the lead singer of the Doors named Jim Morrison? But whatever—the customer is always right. "Cool. Um...peace."

"Nodes of the moon?" Annabelle snaps once he's disappeared onto the boardwalk.

"You don't know about them?" I ask. "It's pretty cool, actually."

"Of course I know about them. I just don't think it's relevant in a ten-minute reading."

I shrug. "Maybe not. But I thought it was at least worth mentioning in case he decides to get his birth chart done later or something."

Annabelle rolls her eyes. "Who's the astrology freak now? Isn't that the whole point of the dare? Can't you see that I won?"

Before I can answer, the door flies open and Sarah stomps in.

"Where have you been?" she asks, glowering at me.

"Um…here? Also at home doing astrology research."

"At home doing astrology research," she repeats, in a tone that suggests I've been mutilating dead bodies in my free time. "Why would you be doing that?"

"Because I run a horoscope business?" I say defensively. "It's cool when you get into it." I shoot a look at Annabelle to see if she'll jump in with her usual defense of astrology, but she is looking as annoyed as Sarah, which I don't get.

"Right," Sarah says, biting off the word. "Well, cool or not, I expect to see you tonight at the rec hall."

"Really? You want me to go to the lame dance?"

She holds up a hand and stares me into silence. "Be there," she says and then storms out, slamming the door behind her and rattling the booth so much that the leaky roof splatters rain on the floor.

"Better do what she says," Annabelle says dryly, straightening the customer forms. "You wouldn't want to get in trouble."

I glare at her. "We have a relationship where there's give and take on both sides," I say, now even more annoyed that she's pushed me to defend the sham. But even as the words come out, I realize that they sound like a joke.

"Some relationship," she mutters.

"At least I'm in a relationship," I snap. This is not my agenda at all. Should I just come out and tell her the truth about her wallet? But she should just know, right? I assumed she did…I'm not doing anything right, which I can totally see in Annabelle's face as her eyes widen and her cheeks flush. "Hey, Annabelle, I—"

"Forget it…you're right," she says. "And here's our next customer."

I spend the next ten minutes telling some tourist named Martin he's been chasing the wrong kind of girl his whole life, and it's time to take a risk and go after a Scorpio or Capricorn and challenge himself to a relationship with someone as stubborn and determined as he is.

"You don't just want to date doormats," I say. "You can handle the challenge of a hardheaded woman."

Martin is nodding like I've just changed his life.

"If you have a gift, you should use it," I conclude.

"You guys are fabulous," Martin says, though really Annabelle just sat there drinking coffee and staring off into space the whole time.

"Thanks. We try. This whole thing was her idea, you know."

"Well, I can see why this is the hot spot on the boardwalk," he says, thumbing through his wallet and pulling out a twenty. "A woman behind me in line drove from three towns over to get a reading."

"Pretty insane," I say, handing him change.

"Listen. I'm having a party Saturday for my eighteenth birthday, and you guys should come. It's going to be a real blowout at the resort—a band, everything."

"Sounds great," I say, glancing at Annabelle, whose face is blank. "We'll be there, right?"

She doesn't even acknowledge me. Instead she smiles at Martin. "Thanks, but I think I'm busy then. Happy birthday, though."

"Well, if you change your mind..." Martin heads out the door.

"Don't ever make plans for me like that again!" Annabelle says angrily.

I flinch. "What? I didn't think—"

"You don't know anything about my life, Pete," she interrupts. With that, she motions in the next customer and refuses to say a word to me for the rest of the day.

And thus begins the Annabelle Lomax silent treatment, which lasts for three straight days. Though I suppose I should have seen it coming. When Leos feel slighted, they tend to overreact.

• • •

By the third day of the silent treatment, I've had it. She needs to grow up already. I swear it's like we're in second grade the way she responds to everything I say with a nod or a shrug. Am I not the one who got her wallet back? Am I not worth the trouble of taxing her vocal cords?

Just when I'm about to slam the door and demand a real, actual conversation, Jed and Daisy stop by. Perfect. I roll my eyes, groan, and flop back into the chair. The loose screw digs into my back. (Another thing: no thanks for volunteering to take the bad chair the last three days, either.)

"Hey guys," Jed says, giving us each a to-go cup of coffee. In all his life, Jed has never made a delivery. Now he's bringing us freebies. The tops of the cups are covered with raindrops from Jed and Daisy's walk over. I don't get it.

"Thanks, this is just what I needed," Annabelle says, as if it's totally natural.

"Yeah, thanks," I say. "But—"

"We wanted you to be the first to know," Daisy says, almost squealing. "We're getting married!"

A couple of people in line cheer.

"That's fantastic!" Annabelle says.

"Totally," I agree.

"It's all thanks to you guys," Daisy gushes.

Jed squeezes her hand. "It's true. I'd still be working my butt off serving coffee alone if you guys hadn't fired up my girl here to ask me out."

Daisy leans over and kisses him. "It was the most important day of my life. We'll have the wedding next summer, and we want you guys to be in it."

"Really?" I gasp.

Jed nods. "Really."

Wow. This is heavy. Heavier than I ever expected for a dare made out of anger. But still...pretty awesome. "I'd be honored," I say truthfully.

There is a silence, and we all look over at Annabelle.

"Um, actually I'm not coming to Gingerbread next summer." She forces a fragile smile. "I'm sorry—but definitely send me pictures and a video."

The rest of the conversation is lost on me. Annabelle isn't coming back to Gingerbread? The summer before college? I can't believe it. It wouldn't *be* Gingerbread without her. And what could possibly keep her away? I mean, I know her Grandma is planning to take her to Greece—but for the whole summer? I'd ask if she was actually talking to me. There is a commotion as Jed and Daisy wave good-bye. Sarah strides in, her eyes flashing.

"So what are we doing tonight?" she asks me, hands on her hips, seemingly oblivious to that fact that everyone in line is staring at her through the door.

"What do you mean?" I begin, with no idea where I'm going. This would be easier without an audience, but everyone is glued in place—even Daisy and Jed, looking back and forth between me and Sarah to see what will happen.

"I'm through with you," Sarah says, hitting each word with emphasis. "I've been wasting my summer with an immature high school boy," she says. "Have fun reading your little astrology charts. I'm going to find a man." With that, she storms out, her feet splashing on the boardwalk.

Did she really say, "I'm going to find a man"? Yes. Yes, she did. I let out a long sigh, not sure whether it's in joyous relief or irritation. Maybe both?

Jed looks at me sympathetically.

"Ouch," I say, rubbing my face for a moment. The atmosphere in the booth is tense, in spite of the fact that I want to leap up and burst into song. "Don't worry," I tell the line of concerned-looking customers. "We got together before I knew our signs were completely incompatible. This will not happen to you."

There's a chuckle from the crowd. A tourist sits down and starts filling out a chart. I sneak a peak at Annabelle and see her face is stiff. I can't tell what she's thinking about what just happened...or if she even cares that she was totally right about Sarah. Or that I'm suddenly single.

"See you, guys," Jed says as he and Daisy walk out.

"Big afternoon, huh?" I say to Annabelle, a shaky smile on my face. After the wedding news and my very public dumping, I figure she *has* to talk—but she shrugs.

And after the next reading, she takes off. Not a word of explanation—she's just gone, leaving me with customers and the booth to clean up. I should have told her the truth about Nate. I should have done a lot of things.

I just hope it's not too late.

Nate Browning

Born September 28: Libra ♎

Rising Sign: Scorpio ♏

You seek harmony and balance in your life and are willing to compromise to get it. Your quick thinking and charm bring people close to you. This is good because you are social by nature. This summer, things may get bad, and be prepared because it's entirely likely they will get worse before they get better. Don't give into your worst tendencies; they'll only lead to ruin.

chapter 14

"Hey there, Birthday Girl!"

Vanessa is so bubbly I'd barely know it was her if my cell phone hadn't identified the caller. I almost didn't answer. I'm not really in the mood to talk. But I'm also not in the mood to be quiet or to get home and stare at the walls of my room all night. So I picked up.

"It's tomorrow," I remind her, sidestepping a puddle on the boardwalk. It's not raining, but the air is heavy after a long afternoon shower. I also notice a real chill in the air. Fall won't be far behind.

"I know, silly," Vanessa coos.

For a second I frown at my phone to affirm that this really is Vanessa talking to me. "Love has turned you into a cornball," I tell her.

She laughs. "I know. Isn't it wonderful?"

"I guess that's one word for it."

"Don't be bitter. Tomorrow you're turning seventeen, and it's your day."

"My day to celebrate the complete suckiness of my life," I reply.

"Are you kidding? You're going to be a senior and rule your nice suburban school where you can have your pick of cute younger guys!"

I shake my head, not believing this is Vanessa, or not wanting to believe it. "So you think my love life is so pathetic it's already time to go the cougar route?" I ask. "And mind you, younger guys in high school are not younger guys in real life."

She laughs. "Okay…so maybe an *older* guy."

"Yeah, I'm sure a gorgeous movie star is just waiting back in Albany to snatch me up," I say. I sit down on a bench and look out over the water.

"So I take it Pete hasn't said anything about your birthday yet," she says.

"He's completely forgotten. It's obvious," I say hollowly. The water is a dark gray under the thick clouds, and the waves are choppy. It perfectly suits my mood.

"You don't believe that," she says.

I take a deep breath. The thing is, I really didn't believe it. Sure, Pete and I are barely speaking, but he doesn't have Sarah keeping him busy anymore. I'm not an idiot. I know he's totally over me. But I admit I was harboring hope that he'd still want to celebrate my birthday with me. Or at the very least *remember* it. But all he can talk about are rising signs being more important than he'd realized, and what it means to be a mutable sign versus a fixed sign. And it's my fault, of course. He can see everyone's birthday but mine.

"Trust me, it's true," I finally tell Vanessa.

"Maybe he'll remember tomorrow," she says.

I shrug. I know she can't see it, but I'm sure she'll get the gist. I mean, yeah, it's slightly possible he'd remember—but considering he hasn't yet, why would he? And at this point, would it really help to have him remember so last second? What makes me ache is that it wasn't important enough to try to overcome our terrible summer and do something together. *I* wasn't important enough.

"I think he's just distracted by his breakup and all," Vanessa says.

Suddenly *I'm* the bitter shrew. "Maybe, but he's better off without her," I say. "Honestly, all he talks about is astrology. It's driving me crazy."

"Wait...*what*?" she exclaims. "How can that drive you crazy?"

"I've decided I hate astrology with a passion," I tell her, even though I know I'm lying.

"Um...got it," Vanessa says. "No astrology for Annabelle."

"At this point, just hearing the word makes me break out in hives."

"I'll let you go," she says, sounding slightly concerned.

"Metaphorical hives," I clarify. "Which are actually worse than real ones."

She laughs. "You should still do something special for your birthday."

"Well, I'm pretty sure my parents are taking me out for breakfast," I say dryly. "So that will be amazing."

"Well, I bet they'll give you good presents." Vanessa is grasping for straws now. "Oh, and I bet Gabe and Grandma Hillary sent you something really terrific! There was an article in the *New York Times* yesterday about silk produced in Central Asia. Maybe they'll bring you a dress or pajamas or something."

I roll my eyes. At least Vanessa is still her true self, even though she's also gaga with new love. "Since they haven't even bothered emailing me for weeks, I doubt it," I say. "They'll probably forget my birthday too."

"Chin up, Little Bear," Vanessa says.

"Um...Did you just call me *Little Bear*?"

"Yes. That is what John calls his little sister. Isn't it cute?"

"Darling," I say. A little bit of misty rain is starting up. I know I'm being a total bummer, but I just can't bring myself to talk to Vanessa about her fabulous boyfriend who adores her and has sweet nicknames for his sister.

"Call me tomorrow," she says. "And remember, there are other fish in the sea. I didn't believe you when you said that after Silas, and look at me now!"

"Right. Bye." I close the phone and walk toward home with the rain falling softly on my face. It's true that Vanessa has found love with another guy, someone way better than Silas. But I know that will not happen to me.

Sure, there may be other guys at some point...guys who make my heart flutter and do nice things for me and maybe even have sweet nicknames for their siblings. But there is only one soul mate, one person I am meant for. And even now, when it's clear he doesn't want me, I know that will never change.

• • •

I can't sleep. After a long night of doing nothing, I figured sleep would be a relief, but apparently relief is not in "the stars." I find myself hating astrology again, and that makes me feel even worse. I've been tossing and turning for an hour, and I'm more awake than ever. I open my eyes and look at the clock. 11:59. It's my last minute of being sixteen, a year that started with such promise. Sweet sixteen. Ha! What does that mean for the year ahead? Sour seventeen?

Of course I can't stop thinking about my birthday last year, that dinner with Pete holding my hand across the table, us laughing the whole night, the way he looked at me like I was something precious and rare. And then, of course, that kiss...

Ugh. I get out of bed as the clock hits midnight. I'm seventeen. Wow, it feels just as bad as I thought it might. I'm going to go crazy staying here so I slip on my beat-up sneakers, throw a hoodie over my pj's, and let myself out of the house as quietly as I can.

At least I have the beach. I love the beach at night. It's so dark, especially with the clouds covering the stars, and the lapping of the waves is comforting in a way I don't even notice in the daylight. It's not raining, so the sand has the crisp gingerbread quality that gave the town its name. It crunches under my feet.

But it doesn't matter…no amount of nostalgia will help. My chest is hollow, and I feel a chill deep inside. I can't believe I'm turning seventeen without Pete by my side. I can't believe there is no Pete in my life, not in a way that means something. Five years of friendship and love gone, just like that. I'd never have believed it was possible, yet here I am.

A drizzle starts up and I didn't bring an umbrella, so I cut my walk short and head to the boardwalk. I'm not ready to go home, and there's an all-night diner where I can get some tea. But as I pass the Star Shack, I suddenly realize I don't want to be around people—even if it's just me and the waitress working the late shift. So I pull out my keys and open the door to our booth.

It looks the same, yet it feels different at night, maybe because it's never empty like this. There's always a line out front, customers bustling in and out, Pete in his chair next to me. At some point he just started sitting in the chair with the loose screw every day, so I think of that as his chair. I look at it as I sit down. It's empty, of course...but in some ways, the Pete memory is closer to me than the real Pete who sits here. I can't believe this all started as a joke...a stupid dare. I stand up, taking in the posters, the tapestries, the pile of astrology books I'd like to burn.

Before I even think it through, I'm taking it apart. The posters rip as I tug them down, but I don't care. They're destined for the garbage anyway, since the last thing I'm bringing home are reminders of this summer. I throw the tapestries into a pile on the floor. They're Gabe's from a hippie stage—so maybe he'll want them (who knows what stage he'll be in after this summer). I'll go ahead and take them home. But the books I pile up with the posters and take outside. It's satisfying to toss them in the wooden garbage shed. No more astrology, no more Star Shack.

Next are the forms, which flutter into the paper recycling and rest gently on top of the books and posters. The pens and clipboards I'll take home. Last are the signs. The paper ones are easy to rip down. The wooden sign—the one I painted first—is harder, but I manage to stand up on one of the folding chairs and tug it off its place above the door. It's too big to fit in the garbage, so I drag it around the back of the diner and toss it in the rusted blue dumpster. A fitting end for it.

I walk back to the booth. It's funny. I thought seeing it empty would make me feel better, but it's only made the cold place in me bigger. It's really over: the Star Shack, the summer, and Pete.

I walk down to the beach, not caring if I get soaked. I didn't know it was possible for anything to hurt this much. I sit on the sand, tears mingling with the rain, not knowing which is which.

Gabriel Lomax

Born January 2: Capricorn ♑

Rising Sign: Cancer ♋

Your genuine commitment to others wins you friends in unusual places. Your down-to-earth approach to your goals generally gets you what you want, though sometimes the solitude that comes with success is not what you seek. This summer, remember to keep trying: even if it seems that all is lost, hope still remains.

chapter 15

I'm up at dawn, but I have a couple of errands to take care of first thing so I'm actually running late by the time I hit the boardwalk, ready for the Star Shack. I was hoping for time to get a cup of coffee. But Annabelle already has a long list of things she's mad at me about...

It's actually sunny out today, and I see a few people lounging on the beach. The sun feels good, but weirdly I miss the gray and the rain. Gingerbread just doesn't feel like Gingerbread if it looks like a real beach.

As I get closer to the Star Shack, I notice a crowd milling around out front. Generally they're lined up, not wandering around...Several of the High-Five dudes are there, baseball caps low over their eyes, looking pissed. Ben and Scott step toward me.

"Dude, what's going on?" Ben asks as I get closer. "Why did you guys close down?"

I resist the urge to tell him he might have had one too many at last night's party. "We didn't close anything—"

"Whatever you say, dude," Scott interrupts, stepping up beside him. "But there's a whole bunch of people out there worried as hell they're not getting their horoscope today." He gestures to the booth. And that's when I notice the sign is gone. Actually, all of the signs are gone. Was our booth vandalized?

Nate, I think. *I bet he came back for revenge…*

I walk closer, ignoring the crowd around me, all the people asking if we're still going to be open today. I can't believe anyone at Gingerbread would trash our booth. Well, except for Nate—but would he really come back? Very doubtful. And as I step inside, I realize what happened.

The Star Shack wasn't vandalized. It was closed permanently by the person who came up with the idea in the first place. And I should have seen it coming.

"Pete, you'll still give me a reading, right?" Scott is asking.

"Um, actually, I think the Star Shack is on…a small hiatus," I say, hoping that will mollify the group. "Sorry. But I'll have more news soon."

"Dude, you better give these people gift certificates or something," Ben mutters.

A mob of angry people wanting romantic advice is the least of my problems right now. I have exactly two hours to find Annabelle. Judging by the finality of what she's done, that is going to be no easy task.

• • •

I start with the obvious, the Opera Café. Jed is serenading Daisy with a full-on aria and doesn't even see me, which is fine. I'm not here to chat. There's no sign of Annabelle, though as I glance around, I remember first seeing her this summer—her curls wild around her face and her green eyes shining with happiness at seeing me.

Now I'm not sure where it went so wrong, but I know I'm desperate to see that look in her eyes. I think about asking Jed and Daisy if they've seen her, just to know if I'm on the right track, but then Daisy joins Jed in a staggeringly awful operatic duet and I flee.

Next I call Annabelle's house. No answer. I knew her parents would be out, of course, but I was hoping things would be easy and she'd just pick up. No dice. I cruise the rest of the boardwalk, hitting Kitty's Clam Shack, where Annabelle dared me to eat a double order of fried clams last year.

Dares, I think. *None of this would have happened except for a stupid dare...*

I remember what I thought about the fried clams; I thought that a dare is a dare so it was worth the stomachache. Little did I know that the clams were questionable and that the stomachache would last three days—but Annabelle felt bad and brought me chicken soup and the sports page every day.

But of course, she's not there. She's not at the diner or Freddy's Fabulous Funnel Cakes either.

Last, I head down to the rides. I scan the Ferris wheel and bumper cars, but there's no cloud of caramel hair to be seen. She's not in the haunted house or at the bouncy tent or at the row of games. As I pass the booth with the basketball nets, I remember two summers ago when we watched a macho guy from Jersey try to win a panda bear for his heavily made-up girlfriend.

She was cheering him on, saying, "Come on, Cowboy. You can do it!" And even though he spent probably fifty bucks, he never managed to sink a shot. Annabelle called me "Cowboy" for a few days after that, until I started calling her "A-Belle" again—and then it was back to "Ski Bum."

Okay, so she's not on the boardwalk. I head over to my car and cruise the spots farther away: the bowling alley, the Everything Beach Store, even Putt a Little. But she's nowhere. I even drive out to the resort I took her to for last year's birthday, thinking maybe she got as nostalgic as I am. But of course she's not there.

Why would she be? I kept my plans a secret too long, so why would she think I remembered her birthday? She probably just thinks I forgot, which is usually what you want when you plan to surprise someone. But in this case, it's about to backfire in a major way.

I rub my forehead, then my temples. How could I have blown things so badly? Did I have to go so far as to hook up with some lame girl and totally ignore Annabelle? And now I'm thinking about something my baseball coach said (which makes it even worse): sometimes I focus so much on the single win that I lose sight of the real victory.

But, hey, what do you know? Surprisingly, like astrology, even my coach is right. Every time I tried to fix it, I just made it worse. I thought if I got into astrology, it would make things up to her—it would show her I was sorry—but instead it just seemed to upset her more. And, if I'm being truly honest, it made me feel good that I was better at it than she seemed to be.

I find myself parking at the resort hotel, walking into the plush lobby. When we were here, Annabelle was wearing a black dress made of silky material...I could barely take my eyes off her. It wasn't that she looked beautiful; she always looks beautiful. It was that she'd dressed up because she knew it would be a special night. She'd put her hair back in these sparkly comb things, and her face was glowing. I couldn't wait to be done with dinner, to be alone with her, so I could finally do what I'd been dreaming of for so long: to kiss her—

Wait.

I know where Annabelle is. I can't believe it took me this long to figure it out. I run out to my car and drive like a madman back to the boardwalk. I park, kick my shoes to the backseat, and then head onto the beach. The sun has been hidden by a thick cloud cover, and the air is thick, ready for a major rain. Our spot is about a quarter mile from the boardwalk, between our houses. And as I squint through the mist, I see: there she is, sitting at the foot of the dune, her face turned away from me.

I'm running now, running to reach her, and when she looks up, I start laughing with relief. I've found her.

"There you are!" I gasp.

She frowns. "You're mad about the booth, right?" she asks.

The what? "Of course not," I whisper. She's still looking all cold and angry, and suddenly the words I really want to say are stuck in my throat.

"Good—because I'm through with it," she says. She starts to walk away.

"Annabelle, wait."

"For what?" she asks. "You want to tell me about my moon sign? Or that you have a new girlfriend? You won the dare. Or lost. I can't even remember anymore. Whatever it is, you still won."

"No," I say.

"What do you mean, no?" she asks, turning up her palms as though she knows I have nothing to offer. "You either proved that astrology is a crock or that you're a genius at it! Either way, I lose!"

I shake my head. The clouds open and I feel the first drops of rain, and in that moment, I know I can do this. I reach out and touch her arm. "I only lose if you walk away right now."

She rolls her eyes. "What is that supposed to mean?"

"Annabelle, I…you win, all right? You win."

She folds her arms across her chest. "Explain how."

"The only explanation is…I love you." I can't believe how good it feels to finally say what I've been feeling for so long—really since that very first day in front of Laser Tag Larry's. Good and painful and very nerve-wracking. But mostly good.

Her eyes narrow. "What exactly does that mean?"

"Exactly what it sounds like."

"Even though you spent the summer dating another girl and barely speaking to me the entire time?" she asks. She takes a step away from me, as though she's going to run away any moment.

"Sarah was…a mistake."

She stares at me.

Finally I'm overcome with both desperation and exhaustion. "Annabelle, I'd give up my Carl Yastrzemski jersey for you, okay?"

And it's finally there: a hint of a smile. "Really?" she asks. "You care to put your money where your mouth is?"

It's a damn good thing I'm wearing said jersey. I rip it off and run for the ocean. But just as I'm about to fling it into the churning water, she grabs my arm, laughing.

"Wait! It's okay. You don't need to do it."

I turn to her and she's close, her hair soft on my arm, and for a minute it feels so good to have her near that I can't even think.

"Are you sure?" I ask when I can form words. "Because I will if you want me to."

She steps in closer, and the smell of her hair and skin intoxicates me. "I'm sure," she says.

And then she reaches up and pulls my face down to hers and kisses me. There's no more mist, no more beach, no more ocean; there is just her body against mine, her lips gentle against mine…just the bliss that is Annabelle. When we finally come up for air, she smiles at me.

"I love you too, Cowboy," she says.

Pete Riley

Born October 21: Scorpio ♏

Rising Sign: Capricorn ♑

You are quick to hide your true feelings, and once hurt, you will keep those feeling completely submerged. But once the right person unlocks your heart, you love deeply, with profound passion and devotion. Stay away from fire signs like Leos, Sagittarians, and Arians, as fire and water do not mix well.

chapter 16

Pete kisses me again, and I feel that familiar shiver, delicious and sweet. His hands are soft against my face, and his body feels strong and warm in the cool rain. I wouldn't have thought it possible, but yes: this is even more incredible than our first kiss. When Pete pulls back and looks into my eyes, I can tell he feels the same. Which makes me very eager for our *next* kiss.

"I have a surprise for you," he says.

I don't wait for him to tell me what it is. I just pull his face down to mine and kiss him again.

"Wait!" After we break away this time, he laughs. "We're going to miss the surprise if we keep this up," he says. He moves a wet strand of hair off my forehead, smoothing it back so tenderly I shudder, then grabs my arm and yanks me toward the boardwalk. "Come with me and you'll see."

"You know I hate waiting," I tell him as we scurry off the damp beach, our fingers intertwined, our hips bumping comfortably together with every step. "Maybe you could just give me a hint?"

"I will say nothing except it's something to mark a very important moment."

My heart swells. He remembered my birthday. Of course he remembered.

We are soaking wet by the time we get to my house, and I figure Pete just wants me to change into something dry before we go to the surprise. I kick off my wet shoes on the porch, then open the door—

"SURPRISE!"

I stagger back into Pete's arms. My living room is filled. John and Vanessa are standing by the door; Jed is sitting on the arm of the sofa with Daisy standing over him, her arms looped around him. And there's Aisha and her boyfriend... It's so crowded I can't even process all the faces—but maybe that's because my attention is caught by the two people coming down the stairs.

"Grandma Hillary!" I shout, running over and flinging my arms around her.

"And what am I, chopped horse meat?" Gabe asks from behind her. He's got a beard going, so I barely recognize him; he truly looks like he's just backpacked the Himalayas. I open my arms and pull him into the embrace.

"Settle down, there," he mutters.

"I can't believe you guys are here," I gasp.

"We got in this morning," Grandma Hillary explains. "Your parents came to pick us up. We'd planned to come home for your birthday and we were going to tell you, but then that young man sent me an email a few weeks ago, asking me to keep it a surprise." She nods toward Pete. "Seems he'd been cooking up this party for some time."

I am so overwhelmed I can't even find words. Pete has been planning this for weeks? As I look around the room, it's clearly true. Of course he has. Punk rock blares from the speakers; everyone I care about has gathered together under balloons, streamers, and a banner that reads: "Happy Birthday, Annabelle and Pete."

"Wait…Your birthday isn't until October," I say as Pete comes up and gives Grandma Hillary a kiss on the cheek. She leads Gabe into the crowd toward a table piled high with cookies, cake, drinks, and presents.

"I flipped the day and month of my birthday so I could be a Leo too," Pete says. "I'm 8/10 instead of 10/8. Much better, don't you think? Leos are meant for each other."

"Well, not really," I say. "Leos have traits—"

"Whatever," he interrupts, looking into my eyes. "*We're* meant for each other. You knew I never really bought into astrology anyway…much."

In answer, I draw him close for another kiss, and the whole room erupts into cheers. We pull apart laughing.

"It's about time!" Jed calls.

"Time for presents," Gabe chimes in, pushing through the crowd with a pile of packages.

"Oh, no," I hear Pete say. He's looking behind the present table at a long, thin package resting against the wall.

"What is it?" I ask.

Pete grimaces. "My parents got me new skis."

I laugh and then remember something. "Were you really going to go skiing with Sarah?" I ask.

"Yeah," he says, rolling his eyes. "Right after I become a Yankees fan."

I knew it, but it's still good to hear. "Where is she, by the way…?"

He shrugs. "Honestly, I have no idea. She texted me saying that she was going home. I haven't heard from her since—"

"Yankees fan?" Grandma Hillary interrupts, wrapping an arm around each of us. "Did I hear you right, Pete? I know I'll see you in a Yanks jersey yet."

Pete grins. "We missed you this summer."

"Well, we saw some beautiful things, but I tell you, there's no place like Gingerbread," she says. "Now who wants to place some bets on the upcoming World Series?"

• • •

After the presents are opened, after Jed and Daisy lead a truly awful operatic version of "Happy Birthday," and after everyone hangs out and eats cake, people begin to trickle out. Soon just Pete and my family are left.

"Time to start cleaning," Pete says.

"No, you're the birthday kids," Grandma Hillary says. "You go have fun. Let us do the cleaning."

We protest but they insist, so Pete grabs our jackets, takes my hand, and leads me to the beach. The rain has turned into a soft mist.

"That was the best birthday ever," I tell Pete, giving him a squeeze with the arm I have wrapped around his waist. "Thank you." The sand is wet under our feet, and waves spill gently onto the shore. It's the perfect Gingerbread evening.

"Thank *you* for putting up with me this summer," he says.

"Well, it wasn't easy…"

"I know," he says, kissing me on top of my head. "So I got you two birthday presents to help make up for it." He reached into his jacket and pulls out an envelope and a flat package wrapped in red paper.

"They'd better be good if you're going to make up for Sarah," I joke.

"Just remember you were the one who had us start the Star Shack," he says.

"But that was kind of fun," I say. "And look how many people we helped with our readings. You *are* a natural. You know that, right?"

"True, true," he says, and I can tell from his cocky tone that he's only half-joking. "But I don't know if I really buy the whole astrology thing in the end. I mean, the stars say we're not compatible."

"Sometimes the stars are wrong," I say, watching a sea gull dive under the water after a fish. "Dead wrong. Honestly, I think *I'm* done with astrology. I'm ready to let the future come and surprise me."

"I'm with you on that," Pete says. "So are you going to open your presents?"

I open up the envelope, and a bunch of tickets fall into my hands.

"Bus tickets from Albany to Mount Snow," he tells me. "I had to spend that Star Shack money on something, so I got the expensive express tickets."

I hug him. "Perfect," I say. And then I turn my attention to the second gift. I rip open the paper and then open the photograph box. Inside is a picture of us at thirteen that Grandma Hillary took. We're standing in front of Laser Tag Larry's. Pete's arm is slung over my shoulder, and we are grinning into each other's eyes, totally unaware of the camera or the people walking by. We are just looking at each other like we've found everything that ever mattered. Because, really, we had.

about the author

When not writing, Lila Castle can be found dancing the tango somewhere in her home city of New York or eating out at her favorite French bistro. She has a number of other interests too, including travel, baseball, exotic hair care products, and of course, astrology.